Love and Legalities

THE AFFAIRS OF LOVE AND COURT
BOOK THREE

JENEVIEVE HERNANDEZ

authorjenevievehernandez.com

Book Cover by Jillian Elyzabeth @jillianelyzstudio

ISBN ebook: 978-1-965713-06-8

ISBN paperback: 978-1-965713-07-5

For my family.
I love you all.

CHAPTER 1
Matteo

It's been one thousand, four hundred and sixty-four days since I broke the love of my life's heart. Exactly four years to the day, and here I am, acting like I'm okay.

I weave through the groups of people gathered around the gardens of The Enchanted Ivy, needing some fresh air from the conversation I was just engaged in. One of the few sore topics I have is when someone brings up the idea of setting me up with someone they know. Something I'll never be able to stomach is the idea of being with anyone except her. Maybe it's because I'm sensitive tonight due to the fact that it's been four years of wondering and pain, but when Mrs. Bray brought up another woman for me, the idea completely sickened me enough to leave the conversation altogether. Sure, most people have no idea that I dated in high school, and they definitely don't know that I will never be over her, but I can't fathom a world where I'm not with her.

Her. My eyes must be weakened by the emotions they've

been carrying all day, because I'm positive I just saw her. How is that even possible? How is it possible that she's merely twenty feet away from me, engrossed in conversation with a group of older women? Just then, as if she senses my gaze on her, she turns, and it feels as though all of the air from my lungs has been stripped, and every sound around me has been silenced.

The love of my life and woman of my dreams, Daniela Lozano, is here. The first girl I ever cared about, and the first girl whose heart I shattered, is here.

CHAPTER 2

Daniela

I knew that the probability of seeing Matteo was high, but I never expected to see him so soon. I haven't properly prepared myself, so here I am, gazing into the eyes of the only boy I've ever loved, wondering how I can flee the situation.

His face is older, and his shoulders are broader than the last time I saw him, but that's to be expected. Four years changes a person. Matteo's ultra-dark eyes are focused on mine, but his body is completely still, not a single muscle moving. In fact, I almost wonder if he's breathing. I know I'm not. Something else I notice, is that he's much taller than me. We used to only be a few inches apart, but he must have grown at least six inches.

I fight the urge to chew my lip, a nervous tic that I've never been able to shake, but I remind myself to keep my composure. Falling apart thirty minutes after arriving at the garden party isn't a good look for the girl who disappeared after high school. For the girl who lost everything four years ago, and came back a completely new person. A new person who built a name for herself, and built back the life that was stripped away in a matter of seconds.

Matteo's gaze is still fixed on me, and I feel tears welling at the corners of my eyes. "Daniela?" He says this as a question, but I know, just like how I knew it was him, that he's certain who I am.

I don't feel like I'm able to respond, but somehow, I manage to push out words. "Yes?"

"Are you really here?" A previous version of myself would have teased him about asking such an obvious question, but I'm barely managing to breathe in and out. I just nod, feeling my hair brush my shoulders as I do so.

"I need to go. I'm sorry, everyone." I finally manage, casting a final glance at Matteo and the women I'm speaking with before quickly walking away. I'm not strong enough to keep myself together throughout the emotions of hurt, love, and betrayal at a formal party. I don't trust myself enough, which is strange, because I've been in so many situations that are much worse.

Matteo is someone who will always be a sore spot for me. There was a point in time when I would have used the word soft, but now, all his name ever brings me is questions and hurt.

CHAPTER 3

Matteo

Quickly turning away after Daniela rushes off, I also retreat to safety. Stumbling through the paths of The Enchanted Ivy, memories of our time here assault me. Memories of us as two innocent seventeen-year-olds escaping to the gardens after parties became too much for us floods my mind, and maybe it's my subconscious that led me to the spot where we spent most of our time. The swing that hangs from the oldest tree on the property still stands strong, and I have to rub my eyes as I turn a corner, because it's as though I can see the memory of me gently pushing Daniela on the swing, with her dress flowing behind her.

Then, the vision changes and suddenly, I'm looking at my sister. "Carmen? Are you back here?" I call out, unsure of what I'm seeing. It almost looks as though she's swinging herself, but I could have sworn I just saw the memory of Daniela and I right where she is. "What are you doing back here, Carmen?" I ask as I approach her, feeling both dazed and slightly worried.

"I was exploring the gardens. Is that not allowed?" She asks softly, stepping towards me.

"Let's get back to the party. You shouldn't be wandering in the dark. You don't know your way around here and could get lost." Is all I'm able to say, the vivid memory of Daniela and I before our world was destroyed still playing in my mind.

After accompanying Carmen back to the main area of the party, I retreat to one of the far benches of the garden, completely unable to even interact with anyone else now. I'm usually much stronger than this, but the only woman I've ever loved is here.

Daniela is here. She's actually here, and not just a figment of my imagination like she has been for the past four years of my life.

CHAPTER 4
Daniela

"So, you saw that boy of yours?" Rena asks me after I've given her a brief rundown of my evening at The Enchanted Ivy. The lines around her eyes and mouth wrinkle as she smiles at her question, as though she's merely asking me for the time.

"I never said that, Rena." I gently say, chewing my lip. Of course, she knows I saw him. Grandmothers are amazing at just knowing things. Well, my grandma, at least.

"But your eyes told me. You have that look you had in high school, Dani." She quips back, her chocolate eyes twinkling.

"Besides, he's not my boy. He's a man, who is definitely not mine. You know that," I say softly, meeting Rena's eyes in the mirror as I speak.

"But he could be yours again," Rena says again, as if that's all it takes. I run my fingers across her hair as I finish braiding the ends of her curly, gray hair.

"I guess so, but he broke up with me, so I'm not going to

just show up and try to date him again. I've moved past him." I finally respond, helping Rena stand from her chair and walk the few steps to her bed. After tucking her in, I give her a kiss on the cheek before praying and reaching over to turn off the bedside lamp.

"You just need to show up in a beautiful dress and show him that he needs to ask you out," Rena whispers just as I step away from her bed.

"Lorena Arango!" I gasp. My grandmother's full name is only appropriate for this situation. "You know I'm not going to do that. You need to get to sleep," I tease, brushing my hand against her forehead as I walk out of her room. My bedroom is right across the hall, just in case she needs me in the night.

When she fell a few weeks ago and fractured her leg in multiple places, bruised some ribs, and had internal swelling, that was finally my wakeup call that I needed to come home to her. Now, I don't know how I was living before having her constant company. It's just like my last year of high school, except this time, I'm taking care of her.

Gliding through the halls and elevator in my building, I exchange greetings with my employees, and soon enough, I'm seated at my desk, with design after design laid out in front of me.

I have an upcoming fall release, with a small winter one just a few weeks later, and I need to get the finishing touches on each winter piece before I send it to the manufacturers. A whole floor in my building is dedicated to manufacturing some of the clothes, since I need to be able to make adjustments to my designs before bulk orders are created. Maybe it's because I started out on such a small scale and had to be hands-on with everything, but even now, I need to know every little detail about everything.

My hands roam over a few sample fabrics as I focus my eyes on the dress design I've been struggling with. One thing that always pulls me out of a design slump is sewing the piece myself, and deciding what to do as I work. I really don't have time for that since I need to send everything to manufacturing in a little over a month, and designing as well as creating will take me time. Especially with Rena's current state of health, and how busy I'm about to be with model casting, so I've been pushing it off. Ideas always flow to me, but for some reason, the final touches on this dress aren't coming to me like they're supposed to.

Remembering what my original objective for coming to the office was, I gather all my designs, computers, and the essentials I'm going to need. Making the decision to create an office at Rena's house so that I can be with her twenty-four-seven was an easy one to make, but actually moving my stuff into the spare, downstairs bedroom and creating a workspace? Not so easy. But it's the best thing for Rena's health, since I don't trust anyone else to spend hours and hours every day with her when I'm not around. She's the only person I have, and I'm going to take care of her in every way I can.

During the drive back to Rena's house, memories of these same roads flit through my mind, one after another. Some by myself—those were mostly spent in tears—and some with Matteo, which also ended in tears. It's almost funny how much of this city my memory holds. I guess only living in one city all your life until college does that to you.

Once I've unloaded everything and placed it all in neat stacks, I start lunch for us, taking careful consideration of the foods the doctors recommended for Rena.

"Rena, are you ready to eat?" I ask as I enter the upstairs living room. Well, that's what we call it, but it's really just the central area of the upper floor that we've added some furniture and a table to, since it's strenuous to help Rena up and down the stairs, since she doesn't want to be in her bedroom all of the time.

"Yes, of course I am," Rena says from her spot on the couch. She has one of her telenovelas playing, but pauses it as I set her food tray on the table in front of her. "This looks wonderful, Dani. Thank you."

"What have you been doing all morning by yourself? Other than watching another soap opera, that is." I tease over my bowl of soup.

"Soap opera? No, no, this isn't a soap opera. This is art. This is..." Rena trails off as she tries to find the right word to convey her message, and I take this as my opportunity to tease her again.

"So, watching his mother try to break them up, and her father forbade their relationship over and over again is art?" I prod. Of course, I watch her telenovelas, too, but Rena has a special love—obsession—for them that is borderline hilarious.

"But it adds to the plot, Dani. You don't get how watching the couple work through every obstacle they face adds to the enjoyment of it." Rena huffs, taking another spoonful of her soup. "You and that boy of yours need to date again so you remember what love feels like." My jaw drops at her words, but truthfully, I'm not even offended by them. I know that she's just doing it to tease me, and that she really didn't mean anything malicious, but her casual mention of Matteo—again—brings back so many memories of us. I was always able to steer the conversation in another direction whenever she'd call me while I was at college and living at my own place, but now that we're having regular conversations all of the time, it seems as though he's all she wants to talk about.

"Well, maybe it's for the best that you're getting your romance fix from your television, because you're not going to be getting it from me anytime soon." I finally respond, patting the back of her hand before eating another spoonful of soup. I feel a sharp pang of guilt, because while I'm acting like I don't care about Matteo, I still do. I would still give him the chance to fix whatever went wrong with our relationship, because I still love him.

"Well, you never actually know when love will come into your life, so I wouldn't be so final about that," Rena says, winking before pressing play on the remote. Of course, I know that love could come to me at any given moment, but it doesn't mean that it will. I saw Matteo at The Enchanted Ivy, and while I never gave him the chance, he didn't just profess his love for me on the spot like in one of Rena's telenovelas. Besides, right now, my main priority is taking care of Rena, and working on new designs for my business. I'm not dwelling on the past, and I'm definitely not still dwelling on Matteo. The first and last boy I'll ever love.

CHAPTER 5

Matteo

I'm still shaken up from seeing Daniela, even though that was a whole week ago. While I've always known that she has this effect on me, I didn't realize that after four years, the pull to her would be even stronger. Everything about her brought back memory after memory of us in high school, and it feels like both nothing and everything has changed.

"Matteo, what do you think of this? I can't seem to figure out if this is something worth considering." Father asks me as I read over the paper he just handed me. We're in his in-home office and going over our weekend list, which are usually things that aren't important enough to take priority at the office in town, so they get pushed to our weekends at home.

"Do they think you'll agree to this? They're asking for

more say in the quarterly assessment, and the strategizing that will be happening there." I say after scanning the paper one more time. "I think that this is pretty much encroaching on the business, rather than a legitimate concern."

"That's what I thought, too. It's better to just say no, right?" Father replies, pulling off his reading glasses to meet my eyes. Of course, I'm grateful that Father trusts my opinion, but it's moments like this one where I find myself questioning whether or not I'm ready for this. All of the classes I took in college and the years of teaching from my father say yes, but the small part of self-doubt within me still creeps in.

"Saying no is the best option. While everyone knows that we're very well-off, they still don't know the exact numbers. We could lose more than half of our investors and still be completely okay. This is just a way for them to get a little bit more voice in the room." I explain. Sure, the business is technically still Father's, but my salary for just being his advisor is more than what most of our investors make in a year.

"Thank you. I'll be sure to let Jane know that she can type up a disagreement to that on Monday." Father says, scratching out a note to himself on the notepad he keeps on his desk. "Which, speaking of, she let me know that her granddaughter has some sort of party the week after next, so she'll be gone for a few days."

"So, you'll be assistant-less and need me to step in?" I verify, glancing at the calendar that hangs on the wall.

"Yes. It should only be a few days, and it's not like you're going to be someone else's assistant, so it'll still be me. In fact, you're practically going to be getting a break from your old man, since it's all computer work." Father replies with a chuckle. I smile at this, even though I don't mind all that much. Father and I occasionally butt heads, but for the most part, we get along very well on both a business and father-son relationship. It wasn't like that until I started working with him every day, since neither he nor Mother made conscious efforts to be involved in my daily life.

"Okay, I'm fine with that. Just let me know what days it will be, and I'll ask her about the schedule." I say, standing from the desk and stretching. "I'm heading down to the gym, but call me if you need me," I say as I leave. After quickly changing into athletic wear, I make my way to the lower floor that has our gym. Equipped with every piece of machinery necessary, it's an industrial-sized gym, all in the comfort of our home.

I'm surprised to see Santiago down here, not because he doesn't exercise, but because he almost never spends his days at home. Rather, he's off with his lousy excuses of friends, or just...out. I acknowledge him, but he hardly even nods back before returning his attention to his set.

CHAPTER 6

Daniela

"You're going to that part tonight, right?" Rena asks from her spot on the couch. I'm currently seated in the large recliner as she watches television, my open sketchbook empty in my lap.

"I'm thinking about it," I reply, looking up from my paper to meet her gaze. "Will you be okay by yourself?" I can leave the house without too much worry, but there are things that Rena can't do by herself, and if she needs me, then I have no problem staying.

"Yes, yes, I'll be fine. There's a new chapter on my show this evening, and I want to watch it in bed, and I don't want you to be all alone tonight." Rena explains.

"Are you saying I'm not invited to watch with you tonight?" I tease, knowing that Rena would gladly have me watch with her later. She's always allowed me to bring my blankets to her bed and watch television for hours until we fall asleep. I guess that's what happens when you're the only two members of your family. You become extremely close, and watch out for each other no matter what.

"Well, if you're asking, then no. You're not allowed." Rena teases back. "I do really want you to be around people your age, though."

"I'll go, but just so you know, I'm pretty much the youngest person to have a membership there. Besides the children of parents who have memberships, there are very few people my age." I tell her. I'm not really sure why I accepted when a membership was extended to me after I moved back, but I figured it couldn't hurt. Deep down, I know it's because I want life to feel like it did before it turned upside down. Before my parents passed, and before the boy of my dreams broke my heart.

"Your boy is there, though? Spend time with him," Rena comments, raising her eyebrows as though this is a very obvious solution.

"Rena, he's not my boy. He hasn't been my boy in four years. You know this." You'd allow him to be your boy again. A small part of my mind whispers, and I can't even refute the thought.

Slipping behind the wheel of my car, I run through my mental list of everything I needed to do before I left. I've already given Rena her dinner, and she's comfortable in bed. The door is locked, and she has her house phone on her bedside table. Everything is ready for me to leave.

The drive to The Enchanted Ivy is short, but Matteo still

finds a way to force his way into my mind. He'll be there, and I'm surely going to see him. My mind mulls over what will happen if he tries to talk to me, and what I'll say. Will he even try to talk to me? Or was one look at me the other night enough for him to remember why he broke up with me?

As I step through the large wooden doors, for a moment, I feel like I'm sixteen years old, and my parents are walking right behind me as I marvel at the interior of the grand building. But the memory fades, and I'm back to being twenty-one, with no one besides Rena in my life, entering the party all alone.

"Daniela, it's nice to see you. I never got a chance to speak with you out in the gardens last week." A woman to my left says, extending her hand. I shake it, and I try to remember who she is, but nothing comes to mind.

"Hello, Ms." I trail off to let her remind me of her name, and she quickly notices that I have no memory of her.

"Renee." She fills in, and as soon as she says this, I remember her. Renee is probably thirty years older than me, but I remember her as one of the less intense women who frequents The Enchanted Ivy.

"Oh, yes, of course. How are you doing?" I respond, smiling now that I've gained my footing.

"I'm doing very well, thank you. Are you enjoying being back?" She asks, leading me to a small group of women.

"It's been lovely. My grandmother and I are enjoying all of the time we've been spending together, and it's nice to be near my office." I reply. I guess a small part of me knew that I would be moving back, and that's why, as soon as it was time for me to expand earlier this year, I decided to move my headquarters here.

"I'm sure she's happy to have you back. I'm already so in love with my sweet grandson. He was born two months ago, and I can't imagine him living far away like you did." Renee comments.

"It's a good thing you have so many more years before he can even think about moving away for college," I say with a smile, unsure of what else to respond with. No one here knows the decisions I had to make at that time, and no one will know the internal battles I faced by myself. We spend a few more minutes talking with the women she brought me to, but once there's a lull in the conversation, I slip away.

I find myself standing near the wall as people around me mingle and chatter, but I can't bring myself to approach anyone. It's not that I don't feel like I belong here, but I don't necessarily feel comfortable, either.

"Daniela?" Matteo's voice is clearer than the last time he spoke, but there's still a question behind his words.

"Matteo?" I ask, turning to face him. There's nowhere for me to run to this time, and I need to face the fact that I'll be seeing Matteo regularly. I can't put off talking to him forever, as much as I would like to.

"You're really here," Is all he says, his eyes flickering to the floor and back to my face. "I'm happy to see you again." I feel my resolve fracture as Matteo speaks; everything from his simple gestures and genuine words brings back a time when he was mine.

"Yeah, I'm back," Is all I manage to get out, internally screaming at how soft my voice sounds.

"How are you doing?" He asks, stepping slightly closer. This is the closest I've been to Matteo since we broke up, and every little detail about him is obvious. If he were to step even closer, I would be able to push back the hair behind his ear and see the tiny freckle that I remember discovering in high school.

"I've been...well. How have you been?" The words are almost easy now, as though it hasn't been years since we've spoken.

"That's good, Daniela. I've been doing well, too," Matteo says quickly, slightly smiling.

That smile.

It brings my own smile to my face as I gaze into his eyes, searching them for something. Anything. "I'm glad you've been well, Matteo, but I think I need to-"

"Daniela, wait, I want to talk to you again." Matteo quickly interrupts, catching on that I'm about to try and end the conversation. It's not that I don't want to talk to him, but I can't be going through all of my emotions in the middle of a party for everyone to see. "Will you talk to me again?" His voice is softer now, and I raise my eyes to his.

"Yes," I finally whisper, knowing that there's no way to avoid this. If I can just show him that there's nothing left between us, since he took a blade to my heart, then I can just peacefully move on, right? "But not tonight, though." Matteo gazes intensely into my eyes for a moment, as though he's working through his schedule in his mind.

"Does tomorrow afternoon work? I'm technically on-call for Father in the morning, but I'll be free all afternoon and evening." Matteo says, and his face and eyes transport me back to our high school days. Something in me can't hold back, and before I know what I'm saying, I lean slightly closer.

"How about you take me somewhere I love, and then

yes, I can make tomorrow evening work." I'm not sure why I'm essentially flirting with him, but it's not intentional. Matteo is bringing out a part of me that I didn't think even still lived within me.

"Absolutely." Matteo agrees, nodding his head quickly. "I'll be at Lorena's house at seven-thirty, tomorrow." His eyes are filled with hope. This is why I'm still drawn to him. I've never seen him look at anyone else the way he looks at me, or act the way he does. I want to be past him, but it's so hard to even think that when I look into his eyes and see every one of my favorite memories dancing in them.

"I'll be there," I say with a nod, clearing my throat. Even though the party lasts for a few more hours, and Matteo doesn't talk to me, since he knows I don't want to deal with all of my emotions here. He doesn't stray far from me, though, either. He's always within twenty feet of me, and it's...comforting. His presence has always felt like a warm blanket wrapped around me, and right now, it feels like there haven't been years of separation between us.

As I slide my light shrug over my shoulders, my eyes meet Matteo's as he continues to watch me. Everything around and between us blurs ever so slightly as my lips part softly. A slow song is being played by the symphony, and my skin erupts in fire as Matteo visibly swallows, his Adam's apple bobbing. Everything from his glowing, golden skin, to his dark brown eyes captures my attention, and for a second, it feels as though this is my first time seeing him. Matteo is the epitome of pure beauty, and if there wasn't a time when I would run my fingers along his sharp jawline and satin-soft hair, I wouldn't believe that he's real. And, here he is, gazing into my eyes with enough smolder to burn the world. As though I'm the only person worth looking at.

An abrupt shift in tone to the song tears me from the silent moment that's stirring between us, and suddenly I feel very exposed. I've been just staring at him as people move around us, and all I can think about is how foolish I must appear. Most people know that Matteo and I have a slight history, like a blip in time, but it was never just that. To most, what we had was something that teenagers all say they have. Love. The only difference is that with Matteo and I, it was real.

Was. That's always the catch when I find myself staying up late thinking about him. To this day, I still don't know why he decided to shatter my heart just mere weeks after my parents were taken from me. Small tears form in my eyes and blur Matteo's face, and the only thing visible is a golden droplet in my eyes as he stays still. Turning quickly, I rush out of the doors, needing fresh air more than ever.

Gasping as hot tears stream down my face, I rest my head against the back of my car seat, so many emotions rushing through my body. How am I supposed to do this? How can I live here and see Matteo everywhere I turn, when I'm still not over him? How can I act as though he's nothing more than a high school memory, when he was my everything? More tears cascade down my cheeks as I allow myself to feel the pain again.

It was easier for me to shove the pain of Matteo down when I was processing my parents' passing, but I've gone through those stages of grief so many times that I know how to process it when something starts to bother me.

Matteo? I tried to forget about him, but that didn't

work, and a part of me knows that it was intentional. Even after all of these years, I still want him. I've always still wanted him, even though he destroyed my heart when I was already at my lowest point in life.

Now, Matteo isn't a need. When we were freshly broken up, I felt as though I still needed him, and couldn't do life without him. I just want him now. I want him to tell me that we still have a future, and that we can fix our past. I want him to remind me that we planned our lives out to be so intertwined with each other's, and that he still wants that. That he still wants us.

CHAPTER 7

Matteo

What have I done? When I saw Daniela, I had to talk to her, even if there was a chance she would turn away and act as though she didn't know me. A small part of me knew that she wouldn't ignore me, since that's not the person she's ever been, but then again, she hasn't responded to the messages and calls I've sent her, either.

I know what I did was wrong, and I knew that before I even broke up with her. But I still did it. I still allowed my parents to have enough control over me to follow along when they said that the love of my life was no longer an acceptable person to date, and eventually marry. It was the stupidest decision of my life to listen to them, but I still went along with it. I still allowed myself to destroy her heart, and then walk away like it was the easiest thing in the world.

That's not who I am, or who I ever wanted to be. I wanted to be her husband, not the man who made her leave town and never look back the second she turned eighteen.

Tossing and turning all night, the thought of seeing Daniela tomorrow sends a thrill through me, but also terror. What am I even going to say? That I regret breaking up with her every day, and I wish to go back in time to change it all? That every moment of every day I still think of her, and wish for a second chance, even though she hasn't spoken to me in years?

Something about Carmen and Santiago is off, but I can't place my finger on it. It's not that they're only being strange with each other, but also, they're being strange with me. Both of them are jumpy and avoidant as we drive into town to run a few errands for Father, and even though I've been somewhat absent as I've been thinking about Daniela and working, I know enough about my two younger siblings to know that they're off.

After a few errands and a surprise trip to grab donuts, we arrive back home, and I work with Father for a few hours before retreating to my room. I know it's usually frowned upon to live at home after college, but it made sense for me. I graduated in two years, and was already working for Father's company, making good money, so it made no sense to move out, especially when I enjoy being around my siblings. And the mansion is large enough that I can go a day without seeing anyone. Secretly, I think the main reason I'm still here is Santiago. He's been so astray recently, and I feel obligated to keep an eye on him until he's standing on his own two feet again.

Carmen, too. Not that she's been astray, but I know what it's like to be the "good" kid, and have the constant fear of frustrating our parents.

Soon enough, it's time for me to leave and see Daniela, and I've already gone through every article of clothing in my walk-in closet, but nothing feels right. Nothing feels enough for her. I'll never be enough for her.

I settle on a cream sweater and trousers, not wanting to be too dressed, just in case Daniela is also in something more casual. If I come overly dressed and she's not matching, then she would surely feel embarrassed. If I come underdressed, then I have no problem with her out dressing me.

Once I'm on the road to Lorena's house—Daniela's grandmother—does every possible bad scenario run through my mind. What if she stands me up? What if she won't listen to me? What if she never talks to me again?

Stop.

Daniela would never stand somebody up, and she always listens to the other side of the story. And, if she never talks to me again, I've already gone four years without speaking to her; a lifetime can't be much different, right? I try to comfort myself as I go over these contradictions to my worries, but all I feel is the pounding of my heart as I think of her.

I can't do a lifetime without Daniela. I already know this, so now I can't go messing everything up when this might be my only chance to explain my side of the terrible story. My side still portrays me in the controllable, weak, and non-confrontational light I was absolutely living within when I broke things off with Daniela, but my hope is that she'll see that I'm not that person, and I will do whatever it takes to prove to her that she is the only woman for me.

Parking in Lorena's driveway, I knock on the front door and wait for a response, and when I do, the air is knocked from my lungs.

"Daniela?"

CHAPTER 8
Daniela

When Matteo speaks, my name a whisper on his lips, I feel all of my self-resolve crumbling. I'm surprised to see that he's in a sweater and trousers, since I figured he might be dressed up a little bit more, but I don't mind the simple outfit on him. That was always something that I enjoyed about Matteo. Even if he had the world at his disposal, he would never flaunt it. Sure, I had the same, but seeing him act as though his family didn't make billions of dollars every year made him more attractive.

"Hi, Matteo," I say softly, opening the door even wider, allowing him to step inside if he'd like to.

"You look breathtaking, Daniela," Matteo says as he steps inside, gently closing the door behind himself. "Your hair, especially." He adds, his eyes traveling over the curls I've gently pinned away from my face.

Matteo has always said that he loves my natural hair, and he was forever grateful when I finally put down the straightener in high school, after almost a year of him asking.

He never meant it in a controlling way; rather, he knew that I was changing it out of insecurity instead of for style. Now, it's been years since I've used heat on it, and I still think of Matteo whenever I style it. I still think of Matteo no matter what I'm doing.

"Thank you, Matteo." I take a breath before meeting his dark eyes again, and every memory of his arms wrapped around me plays in my mind. "What do you have planned for us this evening?"

There's a twinkle in his eyes as he considers my question, and I know that look all too well. "Well, then it wouldn't be much of a surprise. Why don't I show you?" Matteo extends his large hand, and my hand easily slips into it. My knees feel slightly weak as we walk to his car, and my heels click on the driveway, reminding me that feeling weak in three-inch heels won't end well.

We drive in silence for a few moments, but instead of filling it, I allow Matteo to make the first move. The hurt I feel for him breaking my heart pales in comparison to how much I still want to be his, but that still doesn't motivate me to start the conversation.

"Thank you for allowing me to take you out, Daniela," Matteo says after another few minutes, and I can almost feel the nervousness radiating off of him. He does a very good job of concealing it, but even when we dated, I was always able to tune myself into his emotions much easier than anyone else. "You still love sushi, right?" He asks a moment later, as though it's only just now occurring to him that I might have a new favorite food.

"Yes, it's still on my regular meal rotation," I say with a smile, feeling happy that he still remembers the food that I requested every time we went out together. Sure, my love might be a little bit unhealthy at this point, but part of it is still the flavor, and the other part is the nostalgia. Every time I place a bite in my mouth, I'm reminded of the countless takeout packages we consumed together. At one point, near the end of our relationship, we made it a weekly thing to eat sushi on Sunday, which, coincidentally, is today.

I'm not sure if it was an accident, but it's been years, so it would make sense that he forgot about it. I haven't forgotten about it, but I also never acknowledge it, and if I happen to eat sushi on a Sunday, it's not because I'm trying to keep the tradition alive.

"Hopefully you didn't find anywhere better than The Roll while you were away," Matteo teases, and his award-winning smile appears, briefly slowing time for me. How can he still be this gorgeous?

"The Roll, seriously? I'm going to be so overdressed there," I playfully say, glancing down at my blue midi dress and heels, knowing that I will definitely stand out.

"So? You'll be the star of the show like you already are," Matteo replies easily, as though this is one of our high school dates. As though it hasn't been four years since we last talked. "Everyone will be wondering why the beautiful woman in there is being bothered by the man she has in tow."

Heat creeps up my cheeks as his words sink in, and I feel the way I did when we were together. Like Matteo is the only man in the world that matters. "Yeah, I guess so," I say softly, not knowing how else to respond. I'm not supposed to be falling for him so quickly. Well, falling for him at all. I never intended for this evening to deepen my feelings, but here we are, not even to the main course of our evening, and I'm already blushing and forgetting that these past four years even happened.

We enter The Roll, and the familiarity of the orange booths and checkered floors brings on a new wave of emotions. It's as though this is just another one of our Sunday dates, and no time has passed.

I do feel overdressed, but Matteo easily walks next to me as though there's nothing abnormal about us being out together. His hand is painfully close to mine as we order, and the electricity crackling between us instinctively causes my fingers to fidget at my side. I will not take his hand in mine and give in this easily. I'm supposed to be allowing him to talk, not make me fall deeper in love.

"Thank you. We'll have your order over there to table six in a few minutes." The elderly man behind the register says cheerily before turning to deliver our order to the chef.

"Thank you," Matteo says easily, guiding me to one of the far booths. He's just a single stride ahead of me, and I allow myself to admire everything about him. Why must Matteo be the only man I can even look at and find attractive? Why must he so effortlessly have my heart in his hand?

Well, that's the thing, it's not effortless. Everything he did when he was pursuing and dating me was above and beyond anything I could have imagined. Matteo never expected me to just want him, and never thought of himself highly enough to imagine that I would have just fallen at his feet at the slightest indication of him showing me attention. He acted as though he was fortunate to have me give him the time of day, and never let one day go by where I thought he was taking me for granted.

Matteo always had inward self-worth struggles when it came to me, and no matter how many times I assured him that he was the only person for me, he would still go out of his way to show me that even if he was unworthy, he would try every day. Of course, I never once thought that he was unworthy of me, but in some strange way, when he was proving to me that he was worthy of my love, it made him realize that he had desirable qualities, and that he was worthy. After a year or two, I saw such a change in his demeanor as he became secure within our relationship, but more importantly, himself.

Matteo's calm and confident personality had always been buried, but if I'm being honest, his parents never helped him grow his personality; rather, they demanded perfection from him, which is why he became so insecure. It was slow, but watching him grow into the gentleman he became was one of my favorite things about our relationship. Even though we were young by society's standards, we always knew that no matter what, it was him and I.

That is, until he broke up with me mere weeks after both of my parents passed. While I still have some resentment, it's more of a question now. Why?

"I heard that you have a place downtown, now," Matteo comments a moment after we're seated. It takes me a moment to realize that he's talking about the Daniela Lozano building, since Rena's house isn't necessarily in the city, and he's known where her house has been since high school.

"You did?" I respond, meeting his eyes. The deep brown

in his eyes gazes into mine, and a single dark strand of hair falls to his quirked eyebrow. Don't get me wrong, seventeen-year-old Matteo was absolutely gorgeous, but twenty-one-year-old Matteo? He's a whole new level of attractive. If he were an actor, he would be the heartthrob of the century. Secretly, I'm glad his ambitions have never gone past the family company, because knowing that there would be other girls and women dreaming of him rubs me the wrong way.

"It's been the talk of all of the businesses here. I'm proud of you for creating everything you have, Daniela." Matteo answers with nothing but sincerity in his voice. The deep richness in his tone sends goosebumps up my arms, and I fight the urge to act as though him simply speaking causes a reaction.

"Thank you. You've done a lot, too. College in two years and a high-ranking position in a nice company is no small feat." I say softly, tracing my finger on the tablecloth pattern. I can sense that he's about to say something that will contradict me, but before he can respond, one of the waiters brings out our meal and sets the table with the platters of food. Matteo says a quick prayer before we start eating, and I can barely focus on my food.

"I'm not quite sure how to broach the topic, but I would like to talk to you about four years ago. When I…" Matteo trails off as though he's not sure how he wants to say his next words, but it seems as though he just goes with the blunt path. "When I broke up with you. I don't expect you to even understand why I did it, because looking back, I don't even understand why I did. I would just like to explain it, since I left you with a million questions, and that was wrong. Everything I did was wrong." He sounds clear and concise, but after dating him for so long, I know when he's hurting. This is one of those moments, but I am, too. My stomach is twisting itself in knots, and the edges of my vision are becoming hazy.

"Okay," I say softly, unsure of what else to do. Do I really want to relive that terrible time in my life? Do I want to go back to a time when I was in so much pain it was unbearable?

"When I broke up with you, it was because my parents told me I had to," Matteo says, his eyes showing me nothing but the truth. I suck in a deep breath, realizing that my worst fear has just come true. Somewhere in the back of my mind, I'd always suspected that they were involved, but I never wanted to believe it. Matteo had told me they were against our relationship, which was why he kept it on the down low with them. "They found out about us dating a few weeks before we broke up, and they were slowly coming around to the idea, since they didn't think it was that serious." I feel the twisting of my stomach and the spinning of my head stronger now, and barely suppress the feeling of passing out.

"And then?" I ask, not sure what else there is to do. I'm unable to find a reason as to why I agreed to this so early, but now I'm paying the consequences. He taps his fingers on his watch, as if considering something.

"And then a few days before we broke up, we were sitting at dinner, and Santiago said something about us, and they realized we were very serious..." He trails off, and I wonder what he's holding back. This can't be the full story. There's something he's not telling me, and my fingers tingle with nerves. "And they told me I had to break up with you, or leave." He finally says.

"That's not true," I find myself saying, knowing he's not explaining everything. "What else are you leaving out?" My voice cracks because I know this isn't true. Sure, I never doubted that his parents would resent me, but that's not why I know he's not telling me the full truth. I know when he's lying, because he has a nervous twitch, where he fidgets with his watch when he's not being honest.

"I'm not..." Again, he doesn't finish his sentence. That's all the clarification I need. He's not lying yet, but his conscience won't allow him to. So, he's just dancing around the actual reason.

"Yes, you are, Matteo. I know you. I know when you're not being honest, and this is one of those moments. You're holding something back, and until you tell me, I don't want to discuss this. You are welcome to talk to me as a friend, or even an acquaintance, but don't try to bring up this topic until you're going to tell me the truth." I say, standing from our table.

Some deep fight or flight instinct takes over me, and before I know it, I'm outside of the restaurant and at the edge of the parking lot, running right into a man. "I am so, so sorry. I didn't mean to bump into you," I say quickly, looking up into the eyes of someone familiar. "Ryan?"

"Daniela? What a coincidence." Ryan says easily, a smile on his face. "I didn't realize you lived in this area, too." He comments, as though meeting one of your college classmates in an entirely different city is a normal occurrence.

"Yeah, I didn't know you lived here, either," I say, my

eyes shifting to the front door of The Roll. It's a distance away, but an unmistakable figure exits the door, and it's only a matter of time until he sees me. It's not that I'm scared of him seeing me, but I know what he's going to do. He's going to apologize and take me home, but all of the hurt within me will spill over the edge if I have to face him right now. "This is going to sound crazy, but do you think you can drive me home? I'm having car troubles."

Ryan nods, looking surprised, but not bothered by the request. "Yeah, of course, do you want to leave now?" He asks. Glancing over, I see Matteo walking towards us, and feeling reckless and stupid, I say yes, and we both quickly climb into his car and exit the parking lot before Matteo reaches us.

"Thank you, Ryan," I say as I give him directions. I'm too worried about being in a car alone with Ryan, since I had hours and hours of classes in college and a few study groups with him, but being the prepared person I am, no matter the situation, I have a can of pepper spray in my purse.

"No problem. I'm happy to be of help to you," He says easily. "Although, I do have to ask what you were doing out all alone. Hopefully, you wouldn't be asking random strangers to drive you home?" I quirk my jaw at his boldness, but he does have a valid point. I ran right into him in my stupid haste to stop Matteo from not giving me the full story and destroying my emotions.

"I'd rather not discuss it right now, but thank you for your concern," I say politely but firmly. I must have forgotten how blunt and inquisitive Ryan is. To be fair, I didn't pay much attention to my classmates, because I always had my mind on something—someone—else, and was focused on graduating early. Speaking of that someone, my stomach twists at our earlier conversation.

"Of course, Daniela, I was just merely curious," Ryan says quickly. It doesn't go unnoticed that he is essentially asking me again, but I ignore it. Once we've arrived at my house, I quickly exit the car, not wanting him to do anything more for me. I'm grateful, of course, but I don't want him to get the wrong idea.

"Thank you again. Have a nice night," I say just before closing the car door.

"You, too, Daniela. I'm happy to be of service to you. Let me know if you'd like to reconnect again." Ryan calls out his car window before speeding off. It's the right thing to do, since he just drove me home, and I make a mental note to do something with him soon.

"Daniela? Is that you?" Rena calls from her room as I walk up the stairs.

"Yes, I'm back. How are you doing?" I respond, striding into Rena's room to find her still propped up with her pillows, an episode of her television on screen.

"I'm okay, dear, I just wanted to know how it went with your man." Rena practically giggles out her words, and for once, I don't have the heart to remind her that he's not mine.

"It went well, Rena. I'm just super tired and can't wait to climb into bed. I have a lot of work tomorrow." I explain, all of it is true. Tonight has been mentally and emotionally exhausting, and I just need rest.

"Of course, of course. Get to bed, but tomorrow at

breakfast, you're going to tell me everything," Rena says with a wink, turning up the television volume, as if to signal the finality of our conversation. I give her a quick kiss on her forehead before retreating to my bedroom.

What am I going to do?

CHAPTER 9

Matteo

Where is Daniela? Should I leave? Is she still here? What if she were taken?

All of these thoughts plague my mind as I sit in my car, unsure of what to do now. Why didn't I just tell her the real reason why my parents made us break up? I know it's because I didn't have the heart to tell her how terrible the reason was, but maybe I should have just said it anyway?

I dial her phone number multiple times, but just like the hundreds of times I've tried to call her over the years, it goes immediately to voicemail. I type out a message to her, but as soon as I touch the send button, the message says it failed to send. With no other option, I call Lorena's phone, hoping she isn't asleep.

"Hello?" Her voice comes through the line clear, and again, I'm struck by how much Daniela's voice resembles hers.

"Hey, Lorena, I was just making sure Daniela is home safely," I say as casually as possible.

"Yes, she just came inside. Thank you for dropping her off," She responds cheerily, as though it's a normal thing to drop someone off, but then ask if they're home safely. How in the world did she get home? Deciding not to dwell on that at just this moment, I suck in a deep breath.

"Thank you, Lorena. Have a nice night." I say, allowing her to wish me a good night before hanging up.

I sit in the parking lot of The Roll for an unknown amount of time, well past closing hours, and imagine how different the turn of events would have gone had I just told Daniela the heartbreaking truth.

"Matteo, we have a meeting at three, so please be done with those by two-thirty," Father says as I go over the new contracts for an upcoming deal. After these, I still have to go over a board proposal and clean up the notes from this morning's meeting.

"Okay, sounds good," I say, returning to the papers in front of me. As I work, my thoughts return to Daniela, and questions of whether or not she went home alone consume me.

Did she get a driver? Was there someone she knew? Did she just get in a random vehicle, because that was the only other option besides being with me? The thought of Daniela choosing to potentially be in danger rather than be with me sickens my stomach. I know that what I did four years ago was wrong, and I know that what I did last night was wrong. How did I expect to have that conversation with her if I wasn't willing to give her the full story?

I know why I did it, because no one should hear the reasoning my parents gave me as to why I had to break things off, but that doesn't excuse the fact that it was wrong. I need to be honest with her and admit the real reasoning behind our breakup. Of course, it was entirely my fault for complying, but I want Daniela to know that I've regretted it every single day.

The day after I broke things off with her was the day I grew a backbone and took control of my life. That was the last thing my parents had control of, and I wish it hadn't been her. I wish I had realized how weak I was in any other way besides losing Daniela. She was and is the best thing in my life, and I have to show her that I was an idiot at seventeen. Not telling her the full truth last night really destroyed my chances of proving that I'm being one hundred percent honest with her, but I don't think I can tell her the real reason. It would open up wounds so deep within her that I'm not sure she'd ever heal from.

"Matteo?" Father's voice breaks through my thoughts of Daniela, and it takes everything within me not to scowl. I'm not even sure what he was saying, but judging by his slightly irritated face, he's been speaking for a while.

"Sorry?" I say, regaining composure. There is a level of hurt that I hold against my parents for insisting and threatening me to break up with Daniela, but I've grown enough to know that it was just as much my fault as it was theirs. To be honest, I think they think I've forgotten about Daniela. To them, she was just another teenage girl, and not the love of my life.

"I was saying that I just got a call, and we're going to have to stay a little bit late to handle a quick meeting," Father says, his eyebrows lifted as though he's curious as to why I was completely zoned out.

"That's fine, who is the meeting with?" I question, like his announcement didn't just throw off my plans of figuring out a way to apologize to Daniela for the terrible evening I gave her.

"It's with one of the international brands I'm partnering with. For some reason, they got the time zones mixed up, and our live chat meeting will be held much later for us than intended." He explains, tapping his fingers on his desk as if this slightly irritates him.

"I'll be ready for it, don't worry," I say, pushing away from my workspace to stand. "I'm going to head out for some fresh air and lunch," I say, reaching for my bag as I exit the office. I pull out my car keys and use one of the elevators to reach the bottom floor.

I decide on one of the local Mexican restaurants for lunch, even though they'll likely be busy. It's not high-end by any means, but the food is delicious, and sometimes you just need a plate of authentic tacos to work through a terrible twenty-four hours.

Once I've placed my order with the teenager behind the counter, I stand near the pickup area, severely overdressed in my suit and tie compared to the sundresses and shorts around me. My eyes scan the outside of the restaurant, and I have to do a double-take. Daniela?

It's definitely Daniela, but she's with someone else. Another man. He's blond, taller than her, but shorter than me, and definitely our age. Why is she with him? I take three steps towards the door, as if I'm going to do something. What am I going to do? Be a jerk and demand to know why she's talking to another man? What kind of person would that make me?

She's smiling and looking up at him as they stride down the street, and it's all too much for me. I feel my heart beating erratically, and the feeling of nausea creeping in. Who is this man who is capturing her attention and bringing a smile to her face?

They're quickly out of my viewpoint from the window, and it takes all of my self-control not to run out the door and chase after her like I'm in a romantic comedy. I won't ruin her day by barging in on what looks like could be a date, but the urge to throw whoever that was a mile away from her is extremely strong.

While I tried not to picture Daniela dating in college, it was easier to imagine that she wasn't, since I couldn't see it. Here she is now, walking down the street that I frequent, with another man. I know that I have absolutely no "claim" on her, but the sight of her with someone else is sickening. Just like the thought of another woman besides Daniela holding my hand is sickening. I know that Daniela is the only woman for me. I know this for an absolute fact, and nothing will convince me otherwise.

I drive back to the office in silence, the uneaten food on the passenger seat. I couldn't choke it down even if I'd been starved for weeks. How am I going to live my life when there's a probability of Daniela and I not working out and rekindling our relationship?

Stop. Don't think like that, Matteo.

I know myself well enough to know that thinking about a life without Daniela is enough to make me spiral, and I won't be able to concentrate at the meeting taking place in a few minutes.

CHAPTER 10

Daniela

"Thank you, Ryan. I had a nice time at lunch." I say, allowing him to open the car door for me.

"No, thank you. We should go out again," Ryan says, trying to sound casual, but failing miserably.

"I'm quite busy, but maybe we'll be able to work something out," I say politely. A minute later, I'm inside my house, thankful the afternoon is over. It's not that I had a terrible time with Ryan, but he's not Matteo. I went out with him as a thank you for driving me home last night, not because I'm interested in him.

We had a lot of the same fashion classes in college, but unlike me, he didn't graduate early, and still has another year of school left. To be honest, I try to leave all of my college life in the past, because it was the lowest I've ever been, and reliving those memories isn't exactly pleasant.

I mean, the love of my life broke up with me, my parents passed, and Rena was hundreds of miles away. I had no one.

Not a single person there who cared about me, or even checked in every once in a while.

Even though I'm still extremely sad that my parents passed when I was so young, I know that I'll see them again, and I worked so hard to process the emotions and grief. I'm not in any way happy that they're gone, but I can smile at their memory now. I can look back on the amazing seventeen years I spent with them and know that I loved them to the fullest, and they loved me with their entire hearts.

"Daniela, you never told me about last night," Rena says from her position in the recliner. She has a book in her hands, but her reading glasses are resting on her hair, indicating that she hasn't been reading in a while.

"Sorry, Rena. I didn't mean to leave you like that. A college friend is in town and asked me out to lunch, so I had to say yes." This isn't entirely a lie, but I don't like the thought of her getting the wrong idea. Especially since I don't want to think about being with anyone other than Matteo. Although with how big of a Team Matteo fan she is, I'm not sure she'd even like the idea, herself.

"Oh, that's nice. What about that date with your boy?" She prods, not even interested in Ryan.

"It wasn't a date, Rena. We went out for dinner and had a conversation. Nothing else," I say carefully. Rena's doctors advised against upsetting conversations or media, since her fall took a toll on her mental health. Part of the reason I don't want to tell the full truth is because I don't want her to know just how terribly it all went, but also because I worry for her health. She would have a heart attack if she learned that I left Matteo at the restaurant.

"That's it? Come on, Daniela." Rena says this like she's

teasing, but I know she really means it, and isn't satisfied with this watered-down version of the events of last night.

"Rena, that's all. We had a nice conversation and meal, but agreed that we needed to get home early, since we're both busy people." I say, trying to sound convincing. The three bites of food I had were nice, so that's not a lie. And the conversation before the main event wasn't terrible, either. In fact, I would say it was scary how easy it was for us to fall back into our usual rhythm.

"You know you can tell me anything, right? I'm always here for you," Rena says a moment later. Her eyes look a little bit misty, and I know that I've hurt her feelings by being so secretive. Of course, this isn't a production to make me feel bad, but I do. I don't want Rena to feel like I'm intentionally holding things from her, but some things are just better if I regulate what she knows.

"I know, Rena. Why don't we talk about it later today? I need to work on this dress, and time is really running out." I finally say, knowing that I'll come up with a good way to talk about what's going on with Matteo. Besides, I actually do need to work on this dress, because I can't keep pushing out the production date. I've delayed this one so many times, but I know that it will be worth it once I've had the epiphany moment where I come up with the complete design.

Sitting down with the design in the downstairs living room, I allow my mind to work freely and don't put any restrictions on what I'm allowed to sketch. However, that doesn't do the trick. Nothing comes to me, and my mind is completely blank.

Does Matteo think I'm crazy? The thought pops in my head without warning, and after replaying all of last night's events, there's no way he doesn't think I'm deranged. What kind of girl just up and leaves dinner like that, and takes off in a stranger's car? Well, to Matteo, Ryan is a stranger.

My fingers furiously stroke at the blank page as I imagine Matteo sitting alone after I stormed out of the restaurant. What was I even thinking? Of course, I was upset that he wasn't telling me the full truth, but was it so hard for me to listen and maybe work the truth out of him before blowing up and leaving in a rush?

For one single moment, I imagine pulling my phone out and unblocking his phone number. That's the only thing I never allowed myself to do while in college. Not because I didn't want to see if he called or messaged me, but because I wouldn't have been able to restrain myself from calling him. From asking what happened to us, and demanding an answer. Demanding to know why it was so easy for him to shatter my heart and walk away like it was nothing. Like we were nothing.

Focusing my eyes on the sketch in front of me, the design isn't anything like I've done in the past, and I'm not in love with it, but there's a singular detail that sticks out to me. There's a simple pearl design at the cuff of the sleeve, and for some reason, it seems important to the rest of the design. I can't place my finger on it, but the pearls seem necessary to the dress.

CHAPTER 11

Matteo

It's all I can do not to imagine Daniela with another man as I take notes and write down all of the questions I'll need to present to Father after the meeting is over. I have a job to complete, but for some reason, it feels inferior to whatever happened between Daniela and I last night. It feels as though this means nothing if she's decided to move on with another man.

It just doesn't seem like her, though. I can't fathom a world where, in less than twenty-four hours after our date—does it count as a date if she up and left not even twenty minutes into it?—she's out to lunch with another man. Was he potentially the person who drove her home? According to Lorena, she got home safe and sound, and to my knowledge, she doesn't have any friends here. Well, other than the blond man who couldn't keep his eyes off her earlier.

"Matteo, don't you think that's a rather important thing to note?" Father asks quietly, breaking my concentration.

Not that concentration is the best term to use when discussing my previous train of thought.

"Yes," I reply easily, writing down the proposition a board member suggests to the large screen that hosts our live chat with the foreign company we're considering partnering with. It already seems as though most of this deal has already been worked out, but with these things, discussion after discussion is necessary.

The rhythmic beating of my feet on the treadmill is lulling, but it does nothing to ease the clenching in my chest as I think about seeing Daniela in three days at The Enchanted Ivy. There's some sort of celebration for a golf competition, and like everything else, there must be a party to celebrate. I've grown used to the constant social interaction, and if I were more of a businessman, I would thrive there. However, as involved as I am in the business, I don't have that same drive. I know that I'll own the business one day, but the thought of living for the business like my parents do unsettles me. It unsettles me in the same way as imagining a life without Daniela does.

Will I approach Daniela at the party? I want to, but is she completely done with me? Was her leaving me at dinner the final confirmation that she wants nothing more to do with me?

I've never wanted to be the man who says that he's going to wait for the woman to make the first move, but that's really the only thing to do, right? Since she left me, that was her telling me to leave her alone. I can't ask her again to have a conversation with me. That's just harassment. The thought of not doing anything is enough to give me a headache, but I continue to jog, the pumping of my heart drowning out the sound of it clenching in pain at the thought of Daniela.

CHAPTER 12

Daniela

My deep blue dress is the perfect color to highlight my light bronze skin, and the waterfall of curls raining down my exposed back. I'm not sure of the outcome I'm expecting, but I do know that I'm going to see Matteo, and that's enough to send my mind spinning.

Stepping into the large room that hosts the main event of the party, my eyes search the faces for Matteo, and just as I'm about to conclude that he's not here, my eyes land on his smile as he speaks with an older woman, a relaxed expression on his face. I chew my lip for a moment before deciding that it's now or never, and I stride across the room, my gaze only focused on Matteo. Maybe I'm expecting the words to just form as soon as I'm standing in front of him, but if that's what I assumed would happen, I'm sadly mistaken when it's just the two of us face-to-face, and I have nothing to say.

"Daniela, you're-" Matteo starts, but I cut him off before he's even finished with his sentence.

"Matteo, I'm sorry. I shouldn't have left you like that." I

breathe the words out, and there's deep understanding in his eyes.

"No, it's my fault. Don't apologize. You're right about me withholding something, and you were right in feeling upset about being led astray." Matteo says, reaching out and placing his hand on my arm, as if to say, trust me. The touch is electric, and Matteo's face shows that he felt it, too. Although he allows his hand to rest there for another moment before removing it, as if to imply that he's not afraid of our connection.

"Can we have a redo? I want another chance to talk to you, and I'll try not to run away this time." I say softly, peering up into Matteo's eyes, a small laugh escaping me as I finish speaking.

"Of course, Daniela. I'll give you a million chances. As long as it takes for us to get this right." Matteo breathes, his eyes burning with a deep intensity. I smooth my bottom lip across my teeth as I consider Matteo's declaration. Does he really mean that? Does he really want us when we can't seem to get this right? "Do you want to do something tomorrow?"

For a moment, even though this is just what I asked for, I freeze. Can I do this with Matteo? Am I really able to go back to us when we still have all of these problems? Matteo blinks slowly as he gazes down at me, and the part of me that will never stop loving Matteo says yes. I have to do this. "Yes," I finally say. Matteo's lips twitch ever so slightly as he smiles, and I feel the overwhelming urge to reach up and brush my hand across his cheek. What would actually happen? Would he shy away, or would he embrace it like he used to?

"Matteo, come join us!" A man calls to Matteo from a few feet away, completely breaking the electric moment between us. It takes a moment for Matteo to move his eyes from mine, as though he's struggling with the idea of leaving already. Truthfully, I want to imagine us in our own little world where no one can see or hear us, but the polite laughter floating around us is a rude awakening that we're still here in The Enchanted Ivy.

"You should go," I finally say, the words coming out softer than intended.

"Are you sure?" Matteo asks, giving me the option to tell him to stay.

"Yes, Matteo, I'm sure," I say with a small smile, knowing that Matteo is overthinking this. "What time will I see you tomorrow?" I flutter my eyelashes lightly at him, reminding myself that I'm allowed to do this. I'm allowed to flirt and be myself. Matteo stutters for a moment, and I feel the corners of my cheeks rising at this.

"I'll see you at eight tomorrow evening," Matteo says quickly. Too quickly.

"Are you sure?" I question, knowing that he couldn't have possibly just planned something out that quickly.

"Very. You're forgetting I have connections, Daniela. Don't worry about it." Matteo says with a chuckle, turning away from me to join the man who was calling him. Just before he's out of view, he turns and flashes me a wink that sends my stomach fluttering. It's childish, I know, but something about the gesture is so familiar. That was Matteo's thing whenever I was feeling stressed. It was almost his way of saying, "I'll handle whatever happens next," and for me not to worry about it.

The memory of us getting caught kissing by my parents before I told them about us comes to mind, and the memory is so clear that if Matteo looked like a seventeen-year-old just a moment ago, I would have believed we were there again. When my parents found us, they weren't upset, just confused as to why we were together.

"Daniela? Matteo Alvarez?" Mom asked, stepping away from us as we laced our fingers through each other's. She knows of Matteo, but I don't think she's ever spoken to him. Same with Dad. "What are you two doing at the aquarium? And why are you kissing?" She questions, Dad looking equally as confused. I guess they failed to mention that they would also be at the aquarium today.

I glance over at Matteo, unsure of what to say or do. Of course, we're together, but should I say that? Should Matteo say that? He meets my gaze, and a small smile appears on his lips, and he gives me a quick wink before turning to my parents.

"Hello, Mr. and Mrs. Lozano," Matteo says with an overconfident smile, extending his hand to theirs, as though being found kissing your girlfriend by her parents for the first time is a normal occurrence. "I'm Matteo Alvarez." He gulps, and I resist the urge to glance over, unsure of why he's suddenly nervous. "Your future son-in-law." Immediately, all of the air has been sucked from my lungs, and I cough. What in the world, Matteo? We've only been together for a month!

"Oh, well, nice to meet you, Matteo," Mom says, laughter bubbling out of her as she turns to Dad. "Isn't he just

charming, honey?" She says, squeezing Dad's hand. Surprisingly, Dad's face is only amused. I'm not sure what I expected our first interaction to be with my parents as a couple, but this surely isn't it.

"Hello, son," Dad says with a laugh, clapping Matteo on the shoulder. "I guess we'll be seeing a lot more of you now."

"Yes, sir," Matteo responds, chuckling as he does so.

CHAPTER 13
Daniela

"I'm going out with Matteo, Rena. I call into her bedroom before walking down the stairs and into the living room. My open sketchbook greets me from the coffee table and chair near the edge of the room, and I check the clock on the wall before sitting down with it for a moment. I still have fifteen minutes until he'll be here, and just as I pick up my pencil, there's a knock at my door.

"Hey, M-" I start as I open the door, completely stopping when I realize that it's not Matteo. "Ryan?" I say, as though it's a question.

"Hey, Daniela, I just noticed that you left your jacket in my car the other day after lunch, and I figured you'd want it back." He says easily, gesturing to my jacket, which is draped over his arm.

"Oh, well, thank you." I contemplate inviting him, since it's the polite thing to do, but just as I'm about to find a polite way to slam the door in his face, he starts speaking.

"Is there a restroom I can use? Sorry," He asks sheepishly.

"Yes, of course." I find myself saying, letting him in, and showing him to the downstairs restroom. My eyes flick to the clock, and I now have ten minutes to remove Ryan from the property before Matteo is here. I don't want him getting the wrong idea about Ryan, and having him inside my house at almost eight o'clock at night is a great way to do that. Quickly hatching a plan, I walk into my office and rustle a few papers, as if to give off the illusion I'm busy. My outfit isn't by any means simple, but it's not too extravagant either, and I might be able to pull off the idea of staying in tonight.

"Daniela?" Ryan's voice calls from the living room.

"Oh, sorry about that, Ryan. Here, let me get the door for you," I say quickly, leading him from the far edge of the room to the door.

"Well, thank you," Ryan says awkwardly as I essentially push him out the door. "Have a nice night, Daniela."

"You as well," I say with a smile before closing the door. My eyes move to the clock again, and I move to the coffee table where I left my shoes. I just need to slide them on and grab my purse, and I'll be ready to leave. Reaching down to pick up my shoe, my fingers brush over my pencil. I must have dropped it when I answered the door. Thank goodness I found it, because this is one of the few pencils I use for my sketches.

A knock on the door interrupts my thoughts, and I quickly pull on the other shoe and grab the strap of my purse before walking to the door. Opening it, Matteo's familiar face greets me, and a smile appears on my face.

"Hey," Matteo says easily, his eyes moving down my

body, all the way to my feet and back to my face. "You're beautiful, Daniela." He breathes, reaching out to push a single curl behind my shoulder. Matteo's finger lightly brushes my neck as he does so, and instantaneously, goosebumps flood my skin, and I instinctively move into his touch without even realizing it.

"Thank you," I say, gazing through my eyelashes into his eyes as I speak. "You look handsome yourself, Matteo." I'm not brave enough to reach out and graze my fingers across his cheek, but it's not because I'm scared of his reaction. I'm scared of mine. I don't know if I would be able to stop exploring his now-matured face. What would stop me from wrapping my fingers behind his neck and pulling his lips to mine?

"Are you ready to leave?" Matteo says, clearing his throat and removing his hand, as though he's coming to the same conclusion that I just did.

"Yeah, let me just lock the door and I'll be ready," I say, quickly pulling the key from my purse and locking the door behind me. I turn away from the door and almost bump right into Matteo's outstretched arm. Smiling, I slip my arm into the crook of his elbow and allow him to lead me to the car.

"So, what did you plan for us?" I question as Matteo backs out of my driveway. His face is illuminated in the car screen lights, and it washes him in deep blues and greens, giving off a mysterious glow.

"Well, I thought of it at the last minute, but I figured we could go to the aquarium and walk around for a while. Is that okay?" Matteo says with a smile, glancing over for a brief second before turning back to the road.

"That sounds amazing, but shouldn't it be closed?" I question, the idea of it too good to be true.

"To the general public, yes," Matteo replies easily, as though this is common knowledge.

"And we aren't?" I tease, unsure of what exactly he's saying.

"You and I, Miss Daniela, are not the general public tonight. There will only be a few staff members there, but the representative that I spoke with assured me that they wouldn't be interacting with us other than letting us through the opening doors." Matteo says with a grin, flashing me his award-winning smile.

"Well, that's..." I'm at a loss for words. "That sounds amazing. I didn't realize you could pull strings like that."

Matteo's eyebrows furrow for a moment, but he quickly regains his composure. "I usually wouldn't, but tonight is special. You're special, Daniela." He says, his eyes shifting to mine for a split second. There's a deep sincerity in his eyes that I've never seen in a single other person, and I know that he's trying his hardest right now to show me that he's serious about us.

But what is he not telling you? A small voice in the back of my mind whispers, reminding me that we still have so much work before we can be together again. I feel as though there are two sides of my brain, telling me entirely different things at the same time.

One is saying that I love Matteo, and I want him back no matter what, but the other side is reminding me that I still don't know why he broke up with me, and he's intentionally withholding that, therefore I shouldn't trust him.

Ugh, my brain is such a mess, and with everything

happening with Rena's health and my clothing launch that's not finished, a deep feeling of uneasiness has been following me around like my own personal raincloud.

We drive in silence, and it gives me a while to stew in my thoughts and worries. Once we've arrived, Matteo quickly opens my door for me, and like earlier, he doesn't take my hand; rather, he allows me to take his arm. I can't tell if he's intentionally doing this or if it's a reflex for him now. When we were younger, we would giggle every time I took his arm instead of his hand, and we pretended that we were much older, so we had to act properly. On some of our dates, we would only speak in proper English. Smiling as the memories flit through my mind, we walk to the main entrance.

The sky is bathed in an orange glow, and it accentuates the light tan of Matteo's skin. Mine has always been a few shades darker, but Matteo must be spending more time in the sun, because this tan is one I'm not used to seeing. His body is almost glowing, and even though I'm only touching the fabric of his long-sleeve shirt, I still feel the electric buzz between us.

"Well, Daniela, are you ready for our extra special, not open to the general public, date?" Matteo asks as we walk through the doors. The lighting in here is much darker than outside. I have to adjust my eyes for a moment, and once I do, I feel as though we're two Blackstone students who went on a spontaneous date to the aquarium.

"Absolutely."

CHAPTER 14

Daniela

"I've always found the tunnel so fascinating," Matteo comments as we stride through the sea of marine life. The assortment of fish, shark, and coral is enough to make my brain swim, but as we slowly stride through the dimly lit tunnel, I can't help but feel the weight of Matteo's presence.

"Me too," I say softly, the sound of water almost drowning out my voice. "Do you remember when we were here and my parents saw us?" The question pops out of my mouth before I even realize what's happening, and Matteo stops walking altogether.

"Of course I do," He chuckles lightly, and there's a twinkle in his eyes as he does so. "I remember being terrified, but also having this realization that even if I was scared, the feeling had nothing on how I felt for you, and I needed to man up," Matteo answers, gazing into my eyes as he speaks.

"Do you remember what you told my dad?" I whisper, uncertainty clear in my voice.

"I do," Matteo says just as softly. "I still mean it, too.

Never have I considered going back on that, Daniela." His voice is certain, and the butterflies in my stomach swoop as he speaks. This is the Matteo I know. The sure and certain man who isn't afraid of showing me just how he feels.

"You still do?" I need to hear him say it again. Of course, this isn't a proposal of any sort, but it feels like a renewal of a promise. A promise made on teenage love and impulse.

"I do." Matteo says, his voice even deeper than before. "Daniela, I-" Stopping him before he can finish his sentence, I press my index finger to his lips.

"Matteo, I don't want to talk about anything right now. Let's just walk." I say softly. The rush of emotions is too much for me to process, on top of whatever Matteo was about to say. I thread my fingers through his, and Matteo gives me one more longing look before beginning to walk next to me.

After hours of strolling the dimly lit aquarium, we drive back to my house, where Matteo walks me to the door. "I had an amazing time with you tonight, Daniela," Matteo says, brushing his fingers along my neck as he brushes curls behind my shoulder. "When are you available again?"

Sucking in a breath, I lean against the door, my eyes only focused on Matteo's. "I'm really busy with some designs, but if you'd like to do something, I should be free on Monday," I answer, mentally going over the tasks I have in my mind.

"You'll see me in three days, then," Matteo responds, his full smile thrilling. He leans closer to me and wraps his hand behind my neck, bringing his lips to my forehead. My eyes flutter closed, and for a moment, it's only us in the world.

Matteo pulls away and wraps a singular curl around his finger before dropping it and stepping back. "I should probably be leaving. Have a good night, Daniela." Matteo finally says, understanding that as much as we want the night to last forever, that just isn't reality.

"You too," I breathe, meeting his gaze once more. "Drive safely, okay?"

"Always."

CHAPTER 15

Matteo

My car isn't parked in the driveway until five-thirty in the morning, and even then, I have a hard time forcing myself to exit the car and walk through the house, up the flights of stairs to my bedroom. The memory of Daniela's hand in mine is still seared in my mind. This is the most alive I've felt in years. The way we walked for hours without any sense of awkwardness between us was everything I hoped it would be. The way it felt everything like high school, but an enhanced version of us. One where we're both secure in ourselves, but still have the deep longing and want for each other.

I hear Santiago's alarm go off from his bedroom, and for a moment, the idea of him waking up this early sounds strange, until I check my own clock and realize that it's already six-fifteen. It's not abnormal for Santiago to come home late and leave early, but I guess I didn't realize the extent of his comings and goings. At least Carmen isn't sneaking out or anything, like I suspect Santiago is doing on occasion. More than once, I've heard footsteps walk down the hallway to the window, which has a convenient exit route. Not that I would know, of course.

Saturday and Sunday drag, and by Monday, I can hardly contain my excitement to see Daniela. I've made us reservations at a new restaurant in town, and while I'm still not comfortable telling her the reason my parents made us break up, I want to try to explain it to her in a way that isn't directly telling her what they said, but also be more honest. I'm not sure how exactly I'm going to do that, but Daniela does at least deserve to know—to an extent—why I shattered her heart on a random day four years ago.

"Are you going somewhere?" Mother asks as I pass her in one of the large living rooms. Sucking in a deep breath, I turn back to face her. I'm not worried about her trying to make me break up with Daniela again, because I'm fully financially independent—my job at the business is fully contracted—and I'm only living here to spend the last few years before my siblings move out with them, but I'm also not going to be announcing that I'm seeing Daniela again. I want this to be something between just us, because we'll have so many more eyes on us if we're publicly dating. She's becoming more of a household name by the day with her fashion empire, and being the advisor and son of the owner of a multi-billion-dollar company doesn't make me exactly boring either.

"Yes, I'm going out to dinner. Are you doing anything?" I reply easily.

"Oh, well, that sounds nice. I'm just going to be staying in tonight, all by myself. Carmen is out with a friend or something, and Santiago is who knows where. I guess you're leaving, too." Mother answers, as though we're consistently together as a family. Even from a very young age, it was always the three of us together, save for family meals. We've never exactly been a board game in the family room type of family. Father is a workaholic, and Mother is more concerned with her social status than anything else in her life.

"Hopefully you'll get some rest then," I say with a smile, giving her a quick hug before continuing my walk to the door. Checking my appearance one more time by the front mirror, I exit the door and make my way to my car.

Pulling up to Daniela's house, I knock on the door for her. We still haven't spoken about the fact that I'm still blocked from all of her devices, so there's no other way to notify her that I'm here, but I almost don't mind not being able to text or call her. It feels better to be doing everything in person and not give myself the chance to hide behind a screen.

A few moments pass by without an answer from Daniela, and I knock again, assuming she's just coming down the stairs. Frowning when she doesn't answer, I knock again, unsure of what to do at this point. Just as I'm about to knock again, the lock clicks as Daniela opens the door.

She looks frazzled and definitely not ready for a date. Not that she's anything but absolutely beautiful, but I know how she dresses for dates, and this isn't it.

"Hey, Matteo, I'm sorry. I need to call off the date. I'm just super busy, and I don't think this is going to work right now." Daniela immediately blurts out before I can even greet her. What?

"You don't think a date will work out right now?" I feel genuinely confused as I ask this, since she seemed so sure about wanting this. Wanting us.

"Yes, well, no," Daniela says quickly, like her mind isn't completely here. I know this mental state of hers, since she wore it so often in school when she was struggling with a certain topic. "I just need some space right now, Matteo. For now, I can't go on dates with you, and I just need time to...I just need time." No. This isn't happening. I'm not losing Daniela just as I'm getting her back. Things were starting to work with us. This can't be happening.

"Daniela, wait, what did I do?" I blurt out before even realizing what I'm saying. "Did I mess this up? I'm sorry, I don't know how to be better for you, but I'm trying." A single tear trickles down Daniela's cheek, and my heart breaks even more. What have I done to hurt her this badly?

"No, Matteo, it's not you. I have too much going on right now, and we need so much work. I can't dedicate so much time to us when I have this job. And Rena needs my care, and..." Daniela's eyes darken for a moment before turning back to mine. "I'm not saying no forever, Matteo. But I can't do this right now. I need to handle my own things before I can commit to you." She says, like this makes any sense to my shattering heart.

"Is it bad that I don't care if you can commit to me right now?" I say this as lightly as possible, but that doesn't mean that I'm not actually questioning it right now. I've never been rational when it comes to Daniela, and while I know I sound absolutely stupid right now, I can't help it. I've never been able to help it when it comes to Daniela, and I know that I'll never be able to.

"Matteo, you deserve better than that. I can't give you all of me right now, but I can't pretend that you don't mean anything to me, either. I'm so, so sorry that I'm doing this to you, but please understand that I never wanted this to happen, and I didn't mean to do all of this." Daniela apologizes, and as much as I want to plead for more answers, I know that I have to leave. I can't make Daniela do anything else, and even though I'd rather do anything other than turn around, I know that's what Daniela wants, and I'll always do whatever Daniela wants.

"It's not your fault, Daniela. Don't blame this all on yourself," I say softly, giving her my best reassuring expression, but I know she sees right through it. "Have a nice night." A few more stray tears roll down Daniela's cheeks, and I feel an overwhelming urge to brush them off with my finger.

"Matteo, I really am sorry this is happening. I'll see you around, okay?" Daniela's voice sounds shattered, and while I know that this must be hard for her, she's the one making the decision not to pursue anything with me. Why does she sound so broken? Is there something else that's wrong?

"I'll see you around, Daniela."

CHAPTER 16

Daniela

Dropping to the floor once the door has closed, I press my back against it as sobs take over my body. How in the world did this even happen? How did my life spiral so out of my control?

Ryan.

The name feels bitter, and nausea assaults me at the thought of him. Just the thought of him and his disgusting plan is enough to bring on more sobs, but there's nothing I can do to fix this. I can't do anything to stop him because apparently, he's thought out every single way to force me into this.

The memory of him showing up at my front door a few hours ago and calmly explaining his terrible plan to me floods my mind, and I feel my body become even weaker.

Apparently, the other night, right before my date, he saw my design book on the table and took photos of everything. Now, he wants me to appear in public with him and bring publicity to his new clothing brand, since I'm becoming more and more well-known in the industry. If I don't, he's going to accuse me of stealing his designs when I launch my new collection. He wants to be seen in public with me until at least two weeks after my clothing launch. All of this wouldn't scare me as much if I didn't know just how wealthy his family is. Ryan comes from money, and a lot of it. If he were to bring up a legal battle, it wouldn't matter who I hired. Ryan's family is full of lawyers. He made sure to list off each one earlier, and while I was sure he was telling the truth, I did a quick internet search, and they're definitely all legit. It's not that I don't have plenty of lawyers myself, but this is a battle I'll never win.

Now, while I also come from money, it was new money, my parents' money, and every last penny is tied up in a trust until I'm twenty-five. I had to make my own name for myself, and I did it all without using family money to do so.

Rena is from Puerto Rico, and immigrated with her only belongings being her name, and the clothes she was wearing. I don't know much about Dad's parents, but I know they were both from Portugal and moved to the United States right after they got married. As for Grandfather, Rena's late husband, I think he was from Chile. I never knew him since he died well before I was born, but from time to time, I would hear stories about him from Mom or Rena. He's always a sore topic for Rena, since he really was the love of her life, and talking about him immediately makes her tear up.

All of that to say, the business Mom and Dad made was entirely their own, and they had nothing except that. There were no family lawyers, no extra money to fall back on, just their dream and a lot of hard work. They never intended for

Rena and I to be alone, which is why when the first lawyer they hired suggested twenty-five as the age to set trust for, my parents agreed. They continued to add money to the account, and the one thing they added into their contract when they brought in partners and investors was that up until the trust was released to me, a substantial amount of money would be added to the trust each year.

Which leads me all back to Matteo. I can't tell him all of this is happening, because he'll undoubtedly jump in and do everything in his power—which he has a lot of—to fix it, and this is my problem. Also, I can't let Rena know this is all happening. Her doctors have told me that she needs no stress or worry in her life, since she was recently diagnosed with heart issues. This is my problem, and I'm going to handle that, even if it means that I have to be in Ryan's company for the next few weeks.

The thought disgusts me, but what other options do I have? I can just disagree and then have him file a fat lawsuit against me, and then what? I lose my entire business just as we're reaching global success and popularity, because I didn't agree to give some of my hard-earned fame to some loser who can't make a name for himself? Sucking in a deep breath, I wipe the tears from my cheeks and stand, knowing I can't cry about this anymore. This is just the reality of right now, and I have to handle this with as much composure as possible.

As for Matteo, my heart shatters as I see the image of his broken expression when I told him that he had to leave, and this wasn't going to work out between us right now. He looked so happy and excited when I opened the door, but then immediately his face betrayed his emotions and displayed the hurt he was undoubtedly feeling. It took everything I had not to break down right then and there, and even though I'd been fighting off tears before I opened the door, I couldn't hold it in when he started asking what he could do to change my mind. Tears started streaming down my cheeks, and I knew Matteo had to leave before the dam broke.

I know what I need to do, and that's tell him that I'm too busy with my launch to work through our relationship right now, but the idea of pushing him away for a whole month after four years of not speaking to him feels like too much time. There's no other way to do this, though. I can't let him know that Ryan is using me, and with how comfortable I am with Matteo, it will only be a matter of time. Also, I'll be publicly seen with Ryan, and Matteo will have questions that he'll want answers to.

No. I will do whatever it takes to protect Rena, and whatever it takes to protect my dream. As badly as I want Matteo and as much as I love him, Rena's health is the most important thing in my life right now. She's my only living family member, and I'll fight with my last breath to keep her here with me.

CHAPTER 17
Matteo

My vision blurs as I leave Daniela's house, and I can't tell if it's in sadness or anger. Sadness that I've somehow let Daniela down and she feels disappointed with me, or anger with the fact that I just ruin things between us without even trying. I'm not sure what exactly I did, but just knowing that the reasoning behind her needing space is me, sends pulsing rage throughout my veins.

What's wrong with me? Why must I do this to her? Why can't I become the man she wants?

Even though I don't sleep much, when I awake, Daniela is the first thing that crosses my mind. How did last night take such a turn, when I was so sure we were on the right path? Yes, I still haven't told her why my parents forced our breakup, but she never mentioned that when she said she needed a break from us. Was I too much for her so early on, especially when she still doesn't know why I decided to leave her four years ago?

Thoughts tumble around my mind for another hour before it's an acceptable time to be out of bed. I quickly get ready for work, and I mentally list out the things I'll need to do today. There are a few updates from our accountants that I need to go over, and then I need to schedule a lunch tomorrow with a few board members. Lunch isn't exactly necessary, but I want to gently ease them into the idea of the expansion Father and I have been discussing. This isn't our proposal for the idea, but we want to get them thinking about it before we make the official approach.

My suit feels stiffer than it usually does, and my shoes too tight. In fact, everything feels wrong. Nothing in my life feels right after having Daniela so close, and then losing her within the blink of an eye. Again.

Sucking in a deep breath, I exit my room and make my way to the kitchen, knowing that at least some of the chefs will already be preparing breakfast. I'm not in the mood for anything heavy, but there will at least be a few pastries and fruits ready.

I quickly greet the few chefs who are already busy at work as I grab a few pieces of food. The options are eating my food at the table with my siblings, but that will be in an hour. As much as I'd like to spend time with them, I also can't bear another moment in the house. After starting my car and driving to a nearby park, I find a picnic table that still has morning dew on it and set down my water and food. The earthy scent of the trees around me fills my senses, and in the midst of the storms raging in my mind, there's a sense of peace.

I swipe the small bits of earth from my clothes before climbing into my car, and as I drive, instead of the echoing of Daniela's voice from last night, the memory of us in the aquarium floats freely around my mind.

"Good morning, Matteo." The first-floor receptionist says as I walk through the office building, her tone cheerful as she sets up her desk for the day. A few more greetings are called out—being the advisor and son of the owner goes a long way around here—and while I respond warmly to all of them, I'm still not in the best frame of mind.

Thirty minutes later, Father strides into my office, and it's obvious he just arrived. From his still-steaming cup of coffee and slightly tired gaze, I can tell that he's going to be quite irritable today. He doesn't sleep well anymore, and between Santiago frustrating him on the daily, and all of the business issues he needs to keep up with, I know he's tired.

I recently heard him and Mother discussing Carmen, and how she's becoming less and less open with them, and while I can see how that would stress out an average parent, I also know that they're the ones who forced me to break up with Daniela, and the only reason our relationship lasted so long was because of how elusive I was about us. There's no way we would have dated as long as we did if my parents knew the full extent of how deeply in love we were. That's not to say Carmen is in a relationship, but I know where she's coming from, withdrawing from them.

"Morning, Father," I say politely as he steps closer to my desk.

"Good morning, Matteo. What are you working on right

now?" I flicker my eyebrows at his question, but instead of snapping or being rude, I calmly respond. I think last night reminded me just how frustrated I am at my parents for forcing me to break up with Daniela.

"I'm working on the proposal statistics, so that when I bring it up in conversation, I'll be backed by facts and have them all memorized. They'll know a proposal is coming from you soon, but this will give them some reassurance as they think about it all." I respond smoothly, as though we didn't go over this a few days ago.

"Ah, yes, I remember now. Who are you taking again?" Is he losing it? Instead of giving him a pointed look like he should know, I just list off the few men I'll be taking. "Right, right. Thank you. I've been so busy with all of this, and you know how your brother is always sneaking out and getting into trouble," He says, as though I'm supposed to sympathize with him.

"I didn't know he was sneaking out," I say lightly, even though I've been positive Santiago has been leaving at whatever hour he pleases. I do sympathize with Santiago, because I know how difficult our parents are. While I don't agree with everything he's done and I don't think sneaking out is the best idea, I know where he's coming from.

"Yeah, well, it's a real headache to deal with, and we've pretty much given up on trying to do anything about it. That boy is so clever and resourceful, there's nothing we can even do at this point." I inwardly wince. Father and Mother have never been exceptionally good at the whole parenting thing, but it's moments like these that really remind me of how they just don't get their children sometimes.

"I can see how that would be stressful." I do sympathize

with being a stressed-out person, but I don't agree with everything he's saying, especially about my brother. Ever since Santiago's little run in two years ago, he's been so distant and straight-up avoidant of me. He doesn't seem to be the same way with Carmen, but that's also because Carmen knows little to nothing about all of Santiago's struggles.

"You have no idea." Father laments, his eyes sweeping over the papers on my desk. "Anyway, I need to get over to my office. See you at lunch? I was thinking we should go out to lunch today, just you and I."

"That sounds nice. I'll see you at one, then." I say before turning back to my work.

My eyes wander the room for a few minutes after he leaves, and my teeth chew at my bottom lip. What is wrong with Daniela? I know I'm not perfect, nor will I ever be, but was that really enough for her to decide that she can't make this work with us? Is this because of that guy I saw her with? Has he suddenly swept her off her feet, and she's forgotten all about me? I find it hard to believe, but when you know nothing, all you can do is guess as to what's wrong.

I thought that when we had that magical date in the aquarium, that was enough for both of us to realize that we really wanted us to work. Other than my parents, back in high school, we really were perfect together. Of course, we argued here and there, and we had small disagreements and struggles, but overall, we really pushed past every single one of those issues. Until her parents passed.

It absolutely destroyed Daniela, and for those first few weeks, I spent so much time at Lorena's house with both of them as they struggled through their grief. I was more than happy to do it for them. I love Lorena like my own grandmother, and I love Daniela more than anyone else in the world. It was nothing for me to spend every extra second at their beck and call. I would do it all over a thousand times again.

CHAPTER 18

Daniela

"Where are you headed off to?" Rena asks from her seat on the couch. I press my lips together as I realize just how suspicious this looks, and search my brain for a convincing story.

"I have a little business meeting at The Enchanted Ivy," I say easily. It is technically the truth, since this horrible Ryan situation is just business, and I told him that we needed to work out the exact logistics of what he wants from me, because once he specifically tells me, I'm going to do just that and nothing more. I want to get this over with, and then never see his face again. While I absolutely want to avoid a lawyer at all possible, if this goes on past what he tells me today, then even though it terrifies me, I'll get the law involved. I want that to be the very last resort, because a scandal is not what I need right now, but if it gets to the point where I have to protect myself, that's what I'll do.

"That's nice, I saw on the news today that the weather is

really nice. Maybe you should play some tennis while you're out there." Rena comments, smiling earnestly.

"Maybe I will on another day. I might take a stroll on the golf course afterwards," I reply, mulling the idea over. A walk sounds nice, and after dealing with Ryan, I'm sure I'll need a way to decompress.

"Hey, Daniela," Ryan says as I approach the outdoor table he's seated at. I try my best not to scowl, but I don't think the effort went very far.

"Ryan," I reply curtly, sitting down before he can try to push my chair in for me. I don't need any of his politeness, since this whole scheme of his is anything but polite.

Around us, people chatter as they enjoy lunch and conversation, and the gentle chirp of birds does settle the buzzing in my chest. Waiters move from table to table, and when a teenage boy asks us if we'd like a drink, I order a glass of iced tea. Once he leaves, Ryan returns his gaze to me, and I resist the urge to roll my eyes. Something I haven't done in years.

"Thank you for arranging this, Daniela. I know that my measures to gain publicity aren't exactly ideal for you, but surely you understand where I'm coming from." Ryan begins, as though I should be welcoming of his deranged idea. "All I need is for people to see you with me, and when people look into me, they'll see that I'm also a designer, and they'll immediately flock to my business."

"Yes, Ryan, I absolutely know where you're coming from. I did the same thing, too." I say dryly.

"Wait, really? See, I knew you'd understand-"

"Of course I didn't do this. I worked for my own money and made a name for myself without threatening anyone else in the process. I definitely didn't try something this stupid." I finish, cutting him off.

"Oh, well, that's nice and all, but I need to be off the ground with my business within the next few weeks, so some of us need to take more unconventional paths to success." Ryan huffs, as though this makes everything right.

"Well, unconventional is a polite term, but I just don't think that it's the right one. Anyway, give me your exact dates, and I'll go over them with my schedule, and once you've given them to me, you're not going to be changing them." I say, pulling out my planner. "If you try to change anything, I just won't be able to help you. I'm a very busy woman, with a very successful business, and I just don't have the capacity to work in any changes in schedule."

"Well, give me just a moment to look at my calendar, but I hear what you're saying. I don't want to inconvenience you at all." If he were to raise his eyes from his phone, he would be met with my bewildered look, because there's no way he just said that he doesn't want to inconvenience me.

He begins rattling off dates, and as I move my eyes across my planner on the table, my eyes drift to a group of businessmen who are sitting down for lunch. Just before I return to the paper in front of me, my eyes catch on Matteo. He's one of the men in the group who's sitting down for lunch. It's as though as soon as I've registered that he's here, it sends off an alert to him, because his eyes drift to mine. For just a second, there's no one else in the world, but when he shifts his eyes to the pig across the table from me, his gaze narrows.

Of course, this was bound to happen since I'm going along with Ryan's stupid plan, but I didn't expect Matteo to see it all so soon. I don't want him to think that Ryan and I are an object or anything, but I can't exactly deny it, because then that would beg the question of, why else are you spending so much time with him, especially in public. And like I've already decided, Matteo can't know that Ryan is using my own designs against me. I need to handle this myself.

"Daniela, did you hear me?" A grating voice says, drawing my attention back to Ryan.

"No, I didn't. Repeat them," I answer as Matteo gets pulled into a conversation at his own table. Moving my eyes back to the planner, I decide to just push through this right now and work through my feelings on Matteo after Ryan is gone.

I sip my tea as we work out dates that align with both of our schedules, and Ryan rattles off his plans of hiring a few publicists to write about us being seen together. The idea in itself isn't bad, and I have to admit that it will bring even more fame to myself, but I would be happy without this whole situation and less fame, if there were a choice.

My thoughts drift back to Matteo, and I hope that when this is all said and done, he forgives me. I think that he will, but he's going to be upset that I didn't let him help me find a way out of this.

"If that's all you need from me, I have a few investors to meet with," Ryan says, breaking through my thoughts. I resist the urge to comment something about the investors being from his own family. Holding my tongue is one of the first lessons of business my parents taught me, and while I've been in plenty of situations where a snarky comment was my immediate reaction, their reminder to always keep my cards close to my chest always flashed through my mind.

"Have a nice day, then. Hopefully I didn't inconvenience you all too much," I say, taking the last sip of my drink before standing and picking up my purse. My sundress swishes at my knees, and I pull my sunglasses out of my bag.

"Not too much," Ryan replies, as though I actually did inconvenience him. Did anyone teach him manners? Back in college, I wasn't too concerned with the way the students around me acted, but oh, how I wish I had realized just how much of a conniving jerk Ryan is. Learning that early on would have been a big help.

I stride away from the table, and just like Rena promised, the day is perfect. The grass is meticulously cut, and every hedge is trimmed to perfection. The concrete paths around the golf course promise a nice stroll, and I'm thankful I didn't wear extravagant shoes. There are a few older golfers I pass on my walk, but they just give me a simple nod before turning back to their game.

"Daniela, wait!" Matteo's voice calls out to me, and I turn to see him jogging down the path to meet me.

"Matteo, what are you doing here?" I question as he stops next to me. Instinctively, I nervously chew my bottom lip, knowing that Matteo is probably about to ask about my little meeting with Ryan.

"I saw you earlier and wanted to say hi, but you looked busy," Matteo says casually.

"So, you jogged half a mile down this path to say hi?" I tease lightly, as though we can just brush past the whole reason I was busy.

"Well, yes?" Matteo answers, as if he hasn't thought this far in advance. Something I picked up early on about Matteo is that he plans everything out and never misses a beat. Until it comes to me. At first, the idea sounded silly, but the more I learned and knew about him, the more obvious it became.

"Hi," I say softly, looking up to meet his gaze. I'm not sure why I'm allowing myself to do this, but when it comes to Matteo, I just can't say no.

"Hi, Daniela," Matteo replies, his eyes intensely searching mine. We stand like this for an unknown amount of time, but suddenly, as though he's realizing he has to do something, Matteo clears his throat, his Adam's apple bobbing. "What's going on with us?"

"I told you, I'm...busy," I answer too quickly, and while Matteo's eyes look hurt, he doesn't say anything for a moment.

"Is this about the guy you were just with?" Matteo questions. I have to admire his boldness, but it makes my heart beat a little bit faster. The idea of outright lying to Matteo about it makes my head hurt, but what other options do I have?

"No, not really," I answer, convincing myself that I really am busy with other things, and this is just another normal thing.

"But it has something to do with him?" Matteo presses. I know that I would be doing the same exact thing if I were in his shoes, and that's what makes this so much worse. I want to tell Matteo everything, but I can't. Putting my whole business and Rena's health at risk because I trusted someone is my burden to bear, and Matteo isn't supposed to know about it.

"I guess in a way he has a part in it," I finally agree, unsure of what else to say. Matteo's eyebrows quirk, and I know he's holding back on questioning me more, since I'm not offering anything else up. He wants to know everything, but out of respect for me, he's not asking.

Every inch of his skin is glowing in the midday light, and the way his eyes reflect the sun is intoxicating. I feel as though there's an actual magnet pulling me closer to him. Crossing my arms just in case my body decides to move without permission, I meet Matteo's eyes once again. He's so much taller than he was back in high school, and our height difference had been noticeable then. Now, it's almost laughable. I never really thought of myself as short until we started dating, and then in college, I felt normal again, but back in Matteo's presence, I feel exceptionally small.

"Are you going to be walking for much longer?" Matteo asks, completely changing the topic from Ryan.

"I think I'm going to walk until the end of this path, then I'll turn back. Why?" I answer. Everything with Matteo feels so natural, and while I would never give out my plans to walk alone—let alone where I'm going—with Matteo, I don't need to worry. He's so...comfortable to be around.

"No reason, I was just wondering." He replies easily, glancing back to the golfers who have steadily made their way closer and closer to us. "Do you want company?"

"Yes," I answer immediately. Maybe I'll regret this, but I can keep Matteo as a friend for a little bit while I work out this Ryan thing, right? I can tell him that I'm not ready for a relationship just yet, and we can still see each other without it being awkward, and then once this is all behind me, Matteo and I can work on our relationship.

"Really?" Matteo questions, as though he didn't think I'd accept his offer.

"Really."

CHAPTER 19

Matteo

Three days ago, when Daniela and I walked the golf course, everything about us felt normal. Well, as normal as it could be considering she hasn't supplied any information about the guy she was with.

I don't consider myself to be a very jealous man, but seeing her with him again sent my blood racing. Of course, I'm not going to force Daniela to tell me anything, but just knowing who he is would be better than being left in the dark.

She doesn't seem to be dating him, but seeing them out twice together has me really questioning everything. While I'm going to love Daniela forever, the madness I feel when I think about her is overbearing sometimes.

Are all people this crazy over their person? How does the world even work if everyone feels the same way I do about her? Just seeing her is enough to make my brain scrambled, and derail all trains of thought. Like just now, I was cuffing my sleeves in preparation for the party at The Enchanted Ivy, but as soon as I started thinking about her, I completely stopped what I was doing because the thought of her took over my mind.

Both Carmen and Santiago slip away as soon as we're inside The Enchanted Ivy, and while I feel like a slightly bad brother for not even caring where they went, my eyes are already searching for Daniela. I search for her dark curls and tanned skin, but I come up empty. The room around me feels less full knowing that she's not here yet. Well, if she's even coming at all. I hope she's coming.

Couples gravitate to the middle of the floor as slow music fills the room, and I watch as both old and young couples dance together.

"Who are you looking for?" A beautiful voice asks from my side. I turn, knowing my breath is about to be taken away. Daniela's hair is piled into some kind of curly updo, and her dress is a deep shade of red that complements her skin perfectly.

"You." I can't help myself from telling her the truth, and she doesn't look as though she minds. Daniela smiles at this but bites her lip before responding.

"Why?" Her question is simple, but I'm not even sure how to respond.

"I just…" Sucking in a breath, I continue. "I always look for you, Daniela." She doesn't seem too surprised by this, but her face grows softer as she considers this.

"I always look for you, too, Matteo. Even when I don't

think you'll be there." Daniela admits this as though she's telling me something confidential.

"I'll always be there," I say softly, reaching out to brush a few loose curls away from her cheeks.

"Are you sure?" Daniela questions, her eyes meeting mine through her eyelashes. It's a valid question, because I am the one who destroyed our relationship four years ago, but I want her to know that I mean it.

"Even if I'm not sure what's going on between us right now, I'll always be here for you, Daniela. All I've ever wanted is to be there for you." I say, slipping my fingers down her cheekbone, resting my hand under her jaw. Her skin under mine feels like fire, and I swallow the desire for her.

"Do you really mean that?" Daniela's voice holds a layer of insecurity, and it physically pains me to know that I'm the person who caused her to lose trust. I'm the person who broke her, and I sure wasn't there to put her back together.

"Yes." I say softly, gazing intently into her eyes. Feeling a wave of boldness, I move my other hand to hers and take a deep breath. "Will you dance with me?"

"Of course, Matteo." And with that, I slip my hand to her waist and lead her onto the dance floor. Couples all around us evaporate as my hands position themselves on Daniela's hip, her hand meeting mine, and the other resting on my shoulder.

"Are you ready?" I ask, our eyes never leaving each other's.

"Always," Daniela replies, her lips parting into her beautiful smile. Her dimples are showing, and for a moment, my breath catches.

It's been years since I've seen her dimples. I saw them in

my imagination when I would look back on all of the memories of us, but I haven't seen them in so long. They only appear when she smiles with her teeth, and that's something she hasn't done the entire time she's been back. "Are you okay?"

"I'm better than I've ever been." I finally say, my eyes unable to leave the bright smile she's giving me. How did I live life without the sight of her smile?

"Then let's dance." Daniela teases, stepping towards me as the song starts. Something we always did together was dance. We were in the ballroom dancing group back in high school, and granted, we weren't there for very long, but we had so much fun. We also became exceedingly good at it, too.

Falling back into the rhythm of the music, it feels as though no time has passed. Daniela's smile hasn't left her face, and I can feel the smile on my face stretching from ear to ear.

"Do you know what this reminds me of?" I say softly as I pull her back to me after she twirls. Daniela's eyes twinkle before she responds, and the sight of it alone makes my knees feel a little weak.

"Junior year, when we were in the ballroom dancing class?" She teases, bringing herself even closer to me.

"Yes, that, but specifically when we won that award for best couple when we were in that little competition," I say, the memory of us standing on the stage in front of a small board of judges fresh in my mind.

"I do remember that." Daniela muses, tapping her fingers against mine, our secret signal. "I also remember being terrified, because we had the least amount of practice, and thought that we would for sure lose. But then, when I tapped your fingers and told you I completely forgot the dance, you told me the whole dance as we went." She finishes.

"I don't remember that part," I admit, going over the memory a few times. "I was honestly really nervous the whole time, so talking to you probably helped my nerves."

"Even if it was to tell me the dance?" Daniela questions, as though it's strange that would be comforting.

"Absolutely. I was sure I was going to mess up, and going over the steps while I talked to you calmed me down."

"And here I was thinking that I was going to ruin the whole thing by having you tell me all of the steps." Daniela muses, her smile returning as she undoubtedly thinks about our time as dance partners. Once the song ends, we're near the edge of the room, and instead of dancing anymore, we move to a quiet area near one of the far walls under the balcony.

My finger moves up from her hip, and I rest it on her jaw, our eyes completely glued to each other.

"Matteo, are you going to kiss me?" Daniela's question comes out stronger, and for a moment, I'm unsure of what to say. Am I going to kiss her? Until I realize this is a rhetorical question. She wants me to kiss her. So, I do.

CHAPTER 20

Daniela

Matteo's hand slips to the back of my neck and pulls me closer, his lips finding mine as he leans down to my height. His other hand moves on my hip, pulling me even closer to him, our bodies flush. Even though there's my dress between his hand and my skin, I still feel the burn of his touch as though there's nothing in between us.

His lips are as soft as I remember, but there's enough pent-up passion in our movements that I can hardly even take in the softness of them.

For a moment, my hands stay at my sides, but instinct soon takes over, and my hands find their way to his chest, sliding over the lapels of his tuxedo, then finding his shoulders and the hair at the base of his neck.

My hands tangle in his thick, dark hair, and while it's a little bit shorter than how he kept it in high school, it still feels like him. It feels as if I can twist my fingers in it tight enough, nothing will ever pull us apart.

This feels like years of passion and yearning for each

other, all in a kiss. Matteo kisses me like he hasn't kissed anyone in years, and if he's anything like me, he hasn't. Matteo was my first kiss, and I not only want that from him. I want his middle kisses and his end kisses. I want to be the only person in the world his lips find. I haven't so much as held hands romantically with anyone in my life besides Matteo, and I never want to. I never want to learn the creases and feel of another man's hands, let alone lips. I never want to be away from Matteo ever again.

"Someone get them both out of here! What a menace to our beautiful party." A shrill woman screams, voices echoing around the dance across the room. People are huddled in a circle, and while I can't tell what's happening, more and more yelling pulls us from the safe alcove where everything felt like we were the only people in the world.

More and more voices shout, but I can't hear what exactly they're saying, until I hear one familiar voice. Santiago. "Oh, and I'm just-" He snarls before he's cut off by somebody.

"Daniela, I don't want to leave you like this, but I need to see what's happening with him and-"

"Matteo, go see what's wrong with your brother. Don't worry about it." I assure him, pushing his arm gently so he knows that I really mean it.

"Thank you, Daniela," Matteo says quickly before running right through the crowds of people to his brother.

CHAPTER 21

Daniela

Monday rolls around, and I still haven't heard from Matteo. A small part of me is glad that I'm going to get to hold off on telling him that I can't do the whole relationship thing just yet, but an even bigger part of me is slightly worried. What if something truly terrible happened after the party, and now he's unable to get in contact with me?

I could, in theory, unblock his cell phone number, but what if he's changed his number and I end up calling some random person instead of him? That would be going against what I've told myself. Under no circumstances am I allowed to unblock him.

Striding down the stairs in a maxi skirt and camisole, there are three knocks on the door, which both startle and intrigue me. Who would be at my door at ten in the morning? Glancing through the peephole, I can identify that it's some sort of delivery driver. After I open the door, he extends a bouquet of flowers to me, a small note atop the flowers.

"For you, ma'am. Have a nice day." He says before starting back down the path.

Daniela,

Thank you for spending the evening with me on Saturday. I'm so sorry for the abrupt exit I had to make, but I pray you'll forgive me. I know this note is coming a little bit late, but I'd like to take you out tomorrow night at seven. I'll see you then. ~ Matteo

Reality crashes back down as I realize what this means. Tomorrow night, I need to tell Matteo that it was all a big slip-up when I told him to kiss me. Of course, I knew that it was coming, but now it feels much scarier, since I only have all of today and tomorrow to rehearse a stupid speech about how I'm too busy.

Technically, I am, since I have casting for my new models for this launch on Wednesday, and that's a very hands-on program. My assistants have been going through all of the potential models, some well-known and some with no experience at all, but it's up to me to decide who I bring on this launch.

Deep breaths, Daniela. You've been through much worse, and all of this will be behind you soon. I chant to myself, needing the confidence boost, even if it's only from myself.

This is just a few weeks of being out with Ryan, and then after that, Matteo and I will be working on our relationship, and my new launch will be out in the world. I'll be behind the scenes with the next launch, and things will be smooth sailing.

"Hey, Ms. Lozano, will you look this over and approve it?" One of my floor managers asks as I stroll through the casting rooms. I plan on having a variety of women in here on Wednesday, and I need everything to be perfect.

"Let me take a look. What is it?" I say, taking the clipboard from her, quickly scanning the page of notes.

"It's the plan for the models. I have them grouped as diversely as possible, since we have so many different ages."

"What are the youngest and oldest ages?" I don't have control of the approval on who will make it to the initial casting, since there's so much background checking and approvals to do. Also, it gives me the best opportunity to see just the model, and nothing about their background or anything else, if they're just presented to me in the casting room.

"Our youngest is sixteen, and the oldest is forty-five." She says, as though she's already put a lot of thought into the groups.

"And these are the time slots for each group?" I say, glancing over each group and their time tomorrow.

"Yes, I just need your approval so that tomorrow I can have our receptionist send everyone to the appropriate levels and waiting areas." She says, gesturing to the spot below the writing that has a line for me to sign my name.

"This all looks good to me. Thank you," I say, taking her pen and quickly signing my name.

"Thank you. I'll see you on Wednesday." She says, taking back the clipboard and walking down the opposite side of the hall.

I appreciate all of the women I've hired to work for me, because each and every one of them is so talented and constantly moving without my continuous supervision. When I first started hiring people, I quickly found out that while their résumés may have said they were qualified, they weren't ready for the amount of work I expected from them. Now, I have so many amazing women who carry all of the sections I'm not able to manage, and it's a giant weight off my back to not worry about all of the mundane details.

After settling into my office, a message pops up on one of the portals, and it's one of the receptionists asking about a visitor who's requesting to visit my office. Who would be trying to visit me? I reply that she can send the guest up with a security escort, and a few minutes later, there's a knock at the door, and I open it to find the one man who can't stop following me around. Ryan.

Thinking quickly, I invite him to one of my meeting rooms where there's nothing he can photograph and try to blackmail me with.

"Good afternoon, Daniela. I figured I'd come down to HQ and take a look around." He says easily as I tell the security guard he can wait outside the door for Ryan, to guide him back to the exit once he and I are done.

"What do you mean by that? You're not invited here, Ryan." I say briskly once the door is closed,

"Wow, someone's a little feisty this morning," Ryan says

with a chuckle as he sprawls out in his chair, stretching his arms behind his head as though this is his living room.

"Feisty?" I demand, feeling both insulted and disgusted at the same time. "You know, Ryan, maybe you wouldn't need to force me into helping you if you showed signs of someone who wasn't raised in a barn. In fact, raised in a barn is an insult to all of the animals who live in one, because you're a thousand times more disgusting than all of them." I spit out, feeling a rage I haven't felt in a long time take over me. Ryan's jaw goes slack, and for once, he seems to finally realize who he's really dealing with. While I may not have a billion lawyers in my family, my parents and Rena have always told me to stand up for myself. And if this is all I can do right now, then I'll work with it.

"That was quite rude, Daniela. I don't feel I've given you any warrant to treat me so harshly." Ryan begins, stuttering on a few of his words. "I may be going the unconventional route to fame, but that doesn't give you the opportunity to speak distastefully to me."

"Ryan, do you even hear yourself? What did you come here for? I have a busy workday, and being inconvenienced is not how I intended to spend my last few work hours." Ryan never had anything in his clause about being polite to him, and the more he frustrates me, the more I'm going to start using that against him. I'd like to maintain a level of professionalism with him, but with all of the pressure he's placing on me, he's about to be receiving the crumbs of my politeness.

"I just wanted to verify that you're still available for dinner at La Vigne de Miel tomorrow night," Ryan says, his voice more clipped than before.

"Who will be there to write or photograph it?" I question. The restaurant he's chosen is a well-known place for the upper class to dine at, and besides us, there will surely be other high-profile celebrities, as well as businessmen and women.

"Don't worry about that. He's one of the journalists for Chic, so we're going directly to the fashion magazines." Ryan seems excited about this, but the idea of him paying off some journalist to write about him being seen with me rubs me the wrong way.

"And what happens if this story isn't exciting for a little headline on a news outlet?" The question is a valid one, because there's no way that a simple outing with Ryan will be newsworthy.

"Well, I haven't really thought about it that much, since you're quite famous enough, but say this all doesn't work out, then it was worth a shot."

"Ryan, this is a shot in the dark, and you're trying to drag me down in the meantime. You have to understand that I think this is the stupidest plan in the world." I huff. This plan is becoming worse and worse of an idea, and every minute I'm becoming more convinced that it's not going to work.

"You're famous, Daniela! People around the world know all about your little fashion empire! I may have only come up with this plan recently, but it will work." Ryan's voice may be full of emotion, but he's now insulting and shouting at me.

"You may leave now," I say, standing. Walking over to the door and opening it, I gesture for him to leave. "You've been rude and insulting." I bite my tongue, knowing there's a security guard right outside the door. "You need to leave my building, Ryan."

"Daniela, I didn't mean to-"

"Leave."

And with that, my biggest headache is leaving my building. I think of Rena's health and how a legal battle would stress her to the point of a heart attack.

Oh, how I wish to be rid of Ryan for good. Just a few more weeks of this, and then he'll be out of my life for good.

CHAPTER 22

Matteo

After working my way through more than enough agreement details, I finally pass the stack of notes I've made to Father, while he looks them over for bullet points and questions, I gaze out of the floor-to-ceiling window lining his office. From up here, I can see most of the city. Well, most of the upper side of the city.

"I'm going to need a day or two to digest all of this, Matteo. Why don't you take the rest of the day off?" Father says this as casually as possible, but I can't help noticing how old he's beginning to look. Within these last few months, he's begun to seem so much slower, and his ability to work long hours and focus on page after page of papers has dwindled.

"Are you sure?"

"Yes, I'm sure." He says with a dismissive hand wave. I know his health isn't terrible, and he doesn't have a serious problem, but his age is starting to catch up to him. He was already in his forties when I was born, and his sixty-fourth birthday was a few months ago. His age is really just starting to slow him down, which kind of scares me for Carmen and Santiago. Sure, neither of them are exceptionally close to him, but Carmen is barely sixteen.

"Have a good afternoon, Father," I call as I close his office door behind me. At least the extra hour will give me more time to prepare for my date tonight. While I haven't received any kind of confirmation from Daniela about it, I also haven't received any kind of decline, either.

On my drive home, I stop at my house and check up on it, satisfied with the work that's being done.

I decide to get a quick workout in before showering and dressing, and I'm surprised to see Santiago in the gym, too. He has his headphones on and doesn't even notice me getting on the treadmill opposite him. After jogging for a half hour, I call it quits and take my shower and dress.

"What a nice bouquet you chose," The elderly woman behind the counter says to me as I place it in front of her. I chose Daniela's favorites, peonies and dahlias, with a mix of a few other flowers.

"Thank you. Did you arrange it?" I ask as I pull out my wallet to pay her. I try to shop at smaller businesses as much as possible, since having interactions like these with the real creator of the work is so much more enjoyable.

"Yes, of course. I arrange all of the bouquets in here. Is this for a special lady?" She questions as she rings up the price and wraps the flowers. Her look is suggestive as she glances over her glasses, and I feel my neck turning red. Of course, Daniela is special to me, but I can't really discuss the whole backstory of our relationship right now.

"Well, she's very special to me, yes." I offer, stuffing my wallet back into my pocket.

"I see. Maybe you should show her that." The woman suggests, finishing the bow around the stems.

"What do you mean?"

"I mean, if you had to find a workaround to my question instead of saying they were for your girlfriend or wife, then she obviously doesn't know how you feel." She says simply, tucking a little packet of flower food in the folds of the wrapping.

"She does know how I feel." I insist, feeling more and more uneasy.

"Then why aren't you dating or married to her?"

"Because it's...complicated." Does Daniela actually know how I feel? Or does she just know what I've said? My actions four years ago really don't imply she's special to me, and I've been beating around the bush since she's been back.

"Ah, see. You need to show her that she's important to you. Complicated isn't a word in relationships. It either works or it doesn't. And seeing as you're here, you're trying to make it work. Don't just try. Make it work. If this girl wants you, she's waiting for you to do the same." She says, offering the bouquet to me. "Have a lovely day, and thank you for your business."

"You're welcome. Thank you." I say, quickly turning towards the exit. Why isn't this woman working as some relationship coach or something? How did she get into the bouquet business when her relationship advice is actually pretty solid? Well, her bouquets are really beautiful, too.

I suck in a deep breath before knocking on Daniela's door thirty minutes later, and hold my hand with the flowers behind my back. The door opens, and Daniela is wearing a long red dress that highlights her curly hair, causing my jaw to go slack.

"You're so beautiful, Daniela," I say, pulling the bouquet of flowers out from behind my back and extending them to her. "These are for you." Daniela's face isn't what I'm expecting. Her face is between upset and anger, and for a moment, I worry that these are her least favorite flowers, but I know that they can't be.

"I, um, wow. Matteo, these are so beautiful, and you were so kind for bringing them, but I need to tell you that I can't go out with you tonight. I'm so, so sorry." Daniela says quickly, as though the pain she's inflicting will hurt less if she says it faster. "I shouldn't have told you to kiss me the other night. That was a complete mistake, and I regret it."

"You regret kissing me?" The words sound foreign in my own mouth, since this is never something I ever thought Daniela would say.

"Yes, no, let me explain!" Daniela rushes, her mind clearly messy right now. "I don't regret kissing you, but I regret telling you to. I told you that I can't do a relationship just yet, but then I also let you kiss me. I told you to kiss me when I shouldn't have. It gave you the wrong idea, and that was unkind of me. I just can't make this work with you right now, and I'm sorry." Daniela says, her soft face breaking ever so slightly.

"Daniela? Are you ready for our date?" I whirl to find

the same man that I've seen twice with Daniela behind me on the steps. What in the world? So Daniela really can't date me, because she's seeing this guy.

"Ryan! What are you doing here?" Daniela hisses, her neck turning the same shade of red as her dress.

"Picking you up like any decent date would do. Who's this? Is he the guy you ran away from at the sushi place?" What? How does he know any of this?

"Ryan, please go back to your car. Now." Daniela says, giving him such an intense glare that it almost scares me.

"No, that won't be necessary, Daniela. I'll leave you to your date." I say, extending the flowers so she can take them before I walk past Ryan, bumping my shoulder with his as I make my way to my car. It's childish, I know, but I can't help it.

"Matteo, wait!" Daniela calls just as I close my car door. I feel the pull in my chest to go back and allow her to explain Ryan, but for once, I ignore the pain in my chest and just completely move on autopilot.

CHAPTER 23

Daniela

"Ryan, I never agreed to you showing up at my home like that. Leave at once. I will be driving myself to dinner, and you're welcome to meet me at the restaurant." I hiss, pulling my car keys out of my purse, storming past Ryan as I do so.

"Goodness, it's not my fault you and that guy are having some issues," Ryan says, following behind me, his voice careless.

"He's not some guy." I practically yell, spinning so we're almost nose to nose. "He's the love of my life, and the only person I've ever seen a future with."

"Well, you should have mentioned that when you were running away from him on your date. I can't be expected to keep your relationship straight when even you don't know what's happening." Ryan replies, sounding even less caring than before. "Also, Daniela, I was just trying to be considerate and pick you up, but I guess you can't see the kind gesture."

"Ryan, I never wanted a kind gesture. I never wanted

you. But here you are, ruining my life. Right now, legally pursuing you is the only kind of pursuing I want to do with you." I say, turning to my car, climbing in, and slamming the door.

Why in the world did he have to show up and completely destroy Matteo like that? Well, I played a large part in it by really hiding the whole Ryan thing, but now he's going to think that I'm dating Ryan, which couldn't be further from the truth.

Ryan drives ahead of me, but I sit in the driveway for at least thirty minutes before turning the key.

"Right this way, ma'am." The hostess says to me as she gestures for me to follow her to the table Ryan reserved. He's already seated with a drink, but I don't even meet his gaze as I sit.

"Your hair is..." Ryan struggles to find a polite word, since that's what most dates would do, but this isn't a date.

"Ryan, this isn't a date. Stop." I say quietly enough that it would seem as though I'm replying to him, but only Ryan can hear the hiss in my voice. He blinks rapidly, as if he thought I would be welcoming to his advances.

"Try to look like you're enjoying yourself, then. The photographers are set up and will be periodically taking photos." Ryan says, clearing his throat before lowering his eyes to the menu.

"I get to go over the photos before they're officially sent

off to your new outlets, right?" I question, remembering that I haven't asked this yet.

"It doesn't matter to me. I'll try to get them to you a few days before I need the green flag on them." Ryan says, sounding more and more frustrated by this. Good. Maybe he's realizing just how stupid all of this is.

"Thank you."

Within a few minutes, a waitress is taking our orders, and maybe it's wrong, but I intentionally order the most expensive meal on the menu.

This is not happening right now. I look the girl up and down before glancing over at Matteo, and all of the air around me seems to be sucked out of the elevator. Apparently, Matteo's sister, Carmen, is one of the girls who are here for the modeling, and she brought him as her guardian. The look on Matteo's face is frozen, and I know that either he had no idea Carmen was bringing him here to my office, or he at least expected he wouldn't have to interact with me.

I make polite conversation with her, since this isn't her fault, and when she mentions that Matteo is her bodyguard, I do a double-take, but realize that he might actually be that for her right now. The air in the elevator tightens even more when Matteo meets my gaze again. His eyes betray the relaxed body language, and the depths of them bear the heartbreak he wore last night.

After excusing myself from the elevator, I rush to my office to collect myself for a minute, but a portal message pops up, alerting me that the entire group is ready, and I need to start making decisions.

Matteo is waiting in one of the lounge areas of this floor, and I stride past without so much as looking at him. "Daniela, wait." He calls, and the sound of his shoes on the floor stops me. This isn't the right time to try to explain away Ryan, but I can't exactly ignore him, can I? I don't want to ignore him. Turning to face him, he moves closer than most people would in a professional setting, but I don't mind. In fact, I want him to come closer. Even with everything that's happening, I still want him.

"Yes?" I answer softly, pressing the clipboard to my chest.

"I didn't know this was what Carmen was coming for. She just brought this up to me, and I didn't connect the dots until I saw you in the elevator." Matteo says quickly, as though I assumed he planned all of this. "I'm only doing this for Carmen, I promise."

"Matteo, I didn't think you planned all of this, and even if you did, don't worry about Carmen. If this is something she really wants, I'm not going to be unfair because of you." I reply, chewing my bottom lip as he nods his head.

"Thank you, Daniela. This is...important. I think this is her way of trying to make something of herself without the influence of our parents, and I guess it's my job to help make it happen." Matteo says, and I feel a tug at my heartstrings. If I hadn't known Matteo in high school, this wouldn't mean so much to me, but knowing how...controlling his parents are, I know that this must mean a lot to Carmen.

"Okay, I'll keep that in mind. I need to get to work, but why don't you meet me afterward, and we can talk?" Maybe

I'm not sure what I plan on telling him, but I can't let him think that I'm dating Ryan, can I?

Matteo's face brightens, and for a moment, the notion to explain everything washes over me. No. He will try to fix all of this, and there will be a legal battle. Besides the fact that I have good lawyers, Ryan's little fleet of lawyers will rip me apart. Not to mention the fact that Rena's not supposed to be stressed or concerned right now, and this is enough stress to give me a heart attack. I don't even want to think about what this would do to her.

"I'll see you later, then," Matteo says, lowering his gaze to my lips before bringing them back to my eyes.

"See you later, Matteo," I say, my voice coming out much breathier than I expected, and I quickly turn and walk away. What is happening to me? I can't even make up my mind when it comes to Matteo. All I know is that I still want him. All I know is that every time I pass an obstacle on my way to reaching him, another appears.

CHAPTER 24

Matteo

I know I should have brought something work-related to occupy myself as I wait for Carmen, but even if I had, it's doubtful it would have even been opened. Everything about Daniela is replaying in my mind, and the nearness of her earlier still has my brain scrambling. She's the epitome of beauty, and everything I've ever wanted.

Apparently, Ryan knows that, too. There's a part of me that wants everyone in the world to notice and praise Daniela, but most of me wants to be the only person in the world who can see her. I want to be the only person to hear her melodic voice as she speaks, and the only one to coil her curls around my fingers as I kiss her.

Really, I want her. More than I wanted her in high school, if that's even possible. Back then, I only knew her as the girl who was always at The Enchanted Ivy with her parents, and the girl whom I saw occasionally in the school halls. She had the most gorgeous eyes, and the most stunning curls I'd ever seen. She was everything to me. When I finally mustered up the courage to ask her to dance one night, I almost expected her to look me up and down and say no. Instead, she smiled at me and said yes. I didn't know that it was possible to feel my heart pounding in every vessel of my body, until that moment when she took my hand.

Before that, I had no idea just how much I would change, but after that dance, I was never the same. Besides wanting Daniela more than words can describe, I also wanted to be a better version of myself, so that if we did end up together, Daniela would have the very best version of me. She deserves all of that and more, and I've always been more than happy to give her that.

Daniela deserves the sun, the moon, and the stars. She's the most selfless and kind person I've ever met. She's the only person I can see a future with, and I'd give her my dying breath in an instant.

"Matteo, I need to talk to you about something. Last night isn't what it seems like, and I just need to explain it to you." Daniela says as I step into her office. Carmen is waiting in the seating area, and while she has absolutely no clue about our past, she doesn't seem all that curious about us having a private discussion.

"Who is he?" I ask gently. Something about Daniela's expression worries me, but I don't want to seem like the demanding ex who can't stand to see her with another man.

"Ryan is...a friend. We had a business dinner last night, but it's not romantic between us. We met in college, and coincidentally, he's here right now." Daniela rushes, her hair bouncing as she speaks.

"And you regret kissing me because you're busy with Ryan?" I can't help myself from asking the question, even though I know I technically shouldn't.

"No, Matteo. I'm busy with Ryan and a bunch of other things. Rena's health, this new launch, models, all of it. It's too much for me to handle right now." Daniela's eyes betray her words, and I can't tell if it's the part about Ryan being just a friend or about being busy with other stuff.

"It's okay, Daniela," I say softly, hoping she sees the earnestness in my eyes. Sure, I may be upset that instead of going out with me yesterday, she went out with Ryan, but I'm still going to always be here for Daniela, no matter what.

"Really?" Daniela's eyes soften for a moment as they search mine, and I can't help but believe that she's not telling me the full truth.

"Your life is your life, Daniela. You can't walk around worried about everyone else and not take care of yourself." It feels like a death sentence to myself, but she needs to hear it. Daniela has always taken care of others before herself, and while I respect it, it eats her up. There's a difference between making sure everyone around you is cared for, and stressing yourself into illness. Daniela is the latter.

"Matteo, listen to me. I want to take care of you, and I don't want to hurt you. I just need time to fix my life right now." Daniela pleads, as though this is me resigning from my constant longing for her. "There's so much going on, and I can't bring you into it right now. You have to understand that once this is all over, I'll be ready to work on us."

"I understand, Daniela," I say, fully meaning it. I'm the

fool who broke up with her all of those years ago without so much as an explanation. While I want to know what has her so stressed, since I'll do everything in my power to fix it, Daniela doesn't have to tell me anything. She doesn't owe anything to me.

"Matteo, you don't understand-" Daniela breaks off, like she's revealing more than she'd like to, and I bite my tongue before telling her she can talk to me about anything. She knows that already, and I can't pressure her. It's like when she was in college. Yes, at first, I tried to find her and apologize, but I quickly realized that Daniela has to be the one to decide if she wants me. If she wants to tell me what's going on, she will. Until then, I have to be here for her in every way possible. "This isn't anything you've done. This is my choice, and it's not dependent on you."

***

Carmen and I make our way back home, with only a quick stop at the office for a few papers I needed to pick up. Now that I'm home, I can't help but feel disappointed in how my conversation with Daniela went earlier, and how she's hiding something from me. I want her to feel safe with me, like she can tell me everything. Right now, something is wrong. I just can't place my finger on it.

I'm in no position to tell her what she should and shouldn't tell me, because I'm the one who's still hiding the reason why we broke up all those years ago. Daniela deserves the truth about that way more than I deserve to know the truth about what's going on right now, and it's rather hypocritical of me to act this way when I'm still hiding it from her.

My eyes absently skim over the papers in front of me on my desk, but I don't feel like I'm even absorbing a single word from the pages. All I can picture is Daniela's face as she tells me that she can't talk about what's happening right now, and how she's so busy. Even if that's the only reason why she's hesitating to be together, I still want to fix that for her.

I want to fix everything for Daniela, no matter how difficult it might be. She deserves that, after everything, she helped me through in high school, and how she's back here helping Lorena now. Even if she had done nothing for me, I'd still want to do everything for her. She has that effect on me, and I don't know how to escape it. Or, if I even want to escape it.

CHAPTER 25

Daniela

"So, how did it go with your models today?" Rena asks as I set my bag down on the coffee table in front of her. She has her exercise bands in front of her, and she seems to be doing her simple arm exercises. I'm glad to see it, because it's technically my job to make sure she's staying in shape even in the state she's in, and frankly, I haven't been that good of a granddaughter at making sure she's keeping up with them. I make a mental note to check in with her more frequently and keep up with her exercises.

"It went really well. It was a little bit difficult to look past all of their bright and excited faces and get down to business, because I know that I can make or break their dreams, but other than that, it was great." My mind flashes back to Carmen, Matteo's younger sister, and her bright and shining face before we started all of the work. By the end, I could tell she was discouraged, but I wasn't sure what to do. I know she's going to be one of my models, just because of how much she was interested in this.

If I'm guessing, this has to do with their parents, and just like Matteo, she's trapped right now. Maybe she doesn't fully see it, but I know back in high school, Matteo was desperate for something of his own. And, the girl has real talent. Her expressions and the way she moves. Her body is perfect for her age, and what I need. Of course, I don't need anything crazy from the models, but she was everything I needed.

"That's great, honey. I'm really glad you're doing all of this, and it makes me so proud. I know your parents would be extremely proud of you, too." Rena says, her smile accentuating the small wrinkles around her cheeks and eyes, and I reach over and pull her into a hug. "Oh dear. Don't be getting all emotional on me." Rena teases, pulling away after she embraces me for a moment.

"I'm so happy to hear that, Rena. I really missed you while I was in college." I say softly, my eyes moving over her face as I try to picture the three years I was away from her. One of my incentives to finishing college early was to be back with Rena, since she's the only person I have left. I'm not sure how she managed to handle everything around the house while I was gone, but I'm so grateful that she was able to.

"You know I missed you, too, Dani. So much. I'm really happy to have you back, and I hope you never leave. When you get married, don't forget about me." She says with a laugh.

"Rena, you're living with me forever. My husband will be happy to have you. You're going to be a great-grandmother, and be around the kids all the time." I say gently, stroking her hair as I speak.

"I'm glad to hear that. Hopefully, I like whoever you

marry, because otherwise, I'll be such a bother." Rena says with a laugh.

"Rena, I'm sure you'll like him. That'll be one of my deciding factors. If he doesn't like you, he's out." I say with a laugh, my mind flashing to Matteo as I say this. I still picture my future with Matteo, and I know that he loved Rena. Rena loved him. She still loves him.

"You know, Daniela, there is one boy I do like." She says with a suggestive wink. Well, as suggestive as a grandmother can be. "His name starts with an M, and ends with an O," She says, sounding more serious than she did when she was joking.

"Rena! I do know who you're talking about, but right now, things just aren't working between us. It's not him, it's me. I'm too busy with this launch. He knows that, and maybe once everything has calmed down, there will be something between us." I offer, feeling open to discussing Matteo with her now.

"Oh really?" Rena asks, sounding completely intrigued.

"Well, we've seen each other at The Enchanted Ivy recently, and around the city. It's hard to avoid the person you dated for so many years. Especially when you still have feelings for them." I admit, glancing up to meet her gaze. I know Rena isn't surprised by this, but her eyebrows still flick at my open admittance to this. "I feel no different than I did back in high school. If anything, I feel even more for him than I did then, now that I know what the absence of him feels like."

"Daniela, I know life hasn't been easy for you these past few years, but you deserve to be happy, and whether that's with Matteo or somebody else, you deserve it. I think it's with Matteo, and I think you think so, too, but I want you to be happy. You're so strong, and you deserve someone to take care of you, the way you take care of others." Rena says, resting her hand on top of mine. Her hand is soft and warm, and it brings me back to when I was a young child, and she would hold my hand in hers as she told me stories.

"I know, Rena. It's just hard to remember that, sometimes. Deep down, I know that I deserve love, just like everybody else. I deserve to be happy, but sometimes I forget that. Sometimes, everybody else is more important than I am, and I'm happy to give up my time and strength to them." I admit, feeling like a weight has been lifted off my chest. I don't admit it very often, so saying it out loud feels strange.

"You do deserve it. And I think Matteo loves you in that way. I know this sounds like I'm overly affectionate of him, but I'm affectionate of the way he treats you." Rena says gently, rubbing her thumb along the back of my hand. "Matteo talks about you as though you're the only woman on earth, and definitely the only woman he wants. There are a lot of men who refuse to admit that, or even feel that way, but Matteo wears his heart on his sleeve when it comes to you, and I think that something really special." Rena finishes, confirming my feelings on what I think Matteo feels.

"Daniela, you're just so beautiful tonight." A woman says as she approaches me. My eyes lift from the painting that's being auctioned off tonight to glance her way. The Enchanted Ivy periodically hosts silent auctions, and while I don't need or want any of the items they're offering, I place my name down on a few items, if only to remind everyone here that I'm not the same girl who lost everything a few years ago. I shouldn't feel the need to prove anything to anyone, but Mrs. Alvarez's interested gaze as I write my name is enough satisfaction.

"Daniela, I don't think I realized you were here. How are you doing, dear?" She asks, approaching me as though we're best of friends.

"I'm doing well, thank you. How are you?" I reply politely, accepting her quick embrace.

"Oh, I've been well. I've been busy since I'm on one of The Enchanted Ivy boards, but I'm still well. What have you been up to?" Mrs. Alvarez doesn't look as threatening as I remember in high school, but the urge to shrink under her gaze is still relevant. Standing even taller, I push aside the notion.

"That sounds rather taxing. I'm so glad they have someone with as much experience volunteering." I start, noticing how her eyes sparkle at my endless praise, even though it was just the first thing that came to mind. "I've been engaged in my fashion business, and with the ever-rapid expansions, it has been consuming me." I finish, watching her expression shift for a moment.

"Oh? I would love to hear all about it soon. It sounds so fascinating." Mrs. Alvarez says, her eyes moving over to someone to the left of us. Following her gaze, my eyes land on Matteo. He's watching us with a still expression, and I can't decipher the look in his eyes. "So, I guess you've seen

Matteo since you've been back?" Mrs. Alvarez asks, quickly returning my attention to her.

"Yes, a few times," I answer truthfully, meeting her eyes again. There's a flicker of something that looks concerned, but when I don't say anything else, she returns to her curious state.

"That's nice. I'm sure it's been lovely to catch up with your old high school friends." Mrs. Alvarez comments. I can't tell if this is her passive-aggressive way of trying to keep me away from Matteo and in the friend zone, or if she actually means it. Knowing her, it's usually the first option. We never really spent any time together as a couple around Matteo's parents, and while most of the times I was around her, they were less than polite interactions; Mrs. Alvarez occasionally surprised me with being kind. If I were to guess, she's really a good person at heart, but her social status is like a festering wound that only spreads, eating away at healthy flesh.

"I actually haven't seen anyone else besides Matteo," I venture, closely analyzing her reaction. She doesn't look surprised, but there's something else under the mask of her eyes. "To be honest, the last year of high school was very difficult, and by then, Matteo was my only friend. I'm not in contact with any of my other classmates or friends." I finish, clasping my hands in front of my stomach.

"Oh, well, I can see how it might have been difficult at such a young age. I guess Carmen is a little bit younger than you were then?" Mrs. Alvarez muses. I'm not sure if she's saying this for me or herself, but either way, I'm glad she's at least humanizing me now.

"Yes, I think so," I reply, risking one more glance over at

Matteo. He's still watching us intently, as though it's taking everything within him not to walk over here.

"Well, I need to get going, but it was lovely talking to you, Daniela. Let's do it again." And with that, Mrs. Alvarez spins and walks with purpose to her husband across the room.

Resuming my earlier inspection of the painting, I almost don't hear Matteo walk up behind me. Almost. I take a deep breath as I wait for him to speak, and just when I don't think he's going to, Matteo's breath is hot on my neck as he leans down to talk. "What did my mother want?"

Sucking in a breath, but not turning as I respond, I say the most honest thing possible. "She was commenting on the fact that she hasn't seen me recently, and that you and I must be back in contact." Matteo doesn't speak for a moment, and I can almost hear the gears in his mind spinning.

"Did she say anything else?" Matteo asks a moment later. What is he so worried about his mother saying?

"Maybe," I say, finally turning to face him. People are milling about all around us, but the buzz and chatter of them fades into a near silence as I gaze into Matteo's deep eyes. "What do you think she spoke to me about, Matteo?"

"I'm not sure, but you know that my mother is quite... rude at times. If she said anything that offended you, please tell me." Matteo finally says, as though he's willing to push away any of the sugarcoating if that's what it takes for me to tell him if something happened.

"We talked about other things, but nothing uncomfortable. She brought up my parents." I offer, carefully gauging his reaction to this. His reaction is stiff, but his Adam's apple bobs as he swallows.

"What did she say about them?" He ventures, sounding worried about the answer.

"Matteo, why does any of this matter?" I ask, feeling more and more frustrated with how vague and mysterious he's being. Why won't he just tell me the truth?

"Because it matters to me what she says about them." Matteo finally admits, sounding more and more defensive.

"Why? What does she say about them?" I respond, feeling just as defensive as he sounds. Why is his mother talking about my parents? It's not a little-known fact that she was jealous of them, but I thought she would be way past that, considering they've been deceased for four years.

"She doesn't say anything about them, Daniela. Back in high school, she hated them, and at the time, nothing she ever said was polite. I don't want her to be saying anything like that now." Matteo finally gives in, pressing his lips together after he finishes speaking.

"What did she say?"

"Daniela, we can't talk about this right now. If she really didn't say anything, then we need to have this discussion elsewhere." Matteo says, sounding not quite frustrated, but like he can't discuss it further with me in this room.

"What do you mean by have it elsewhere? What are you not telling me?" I whisper, feeling suddenly very insecure, knowing that my parents have been a harsh topic at his house.

"It's not that, Daniela. We just can't talk about it here, okay?" Matteo says, glancing over his shoulder as people move around us.

"Matteo, I don't know what's going on, but you're going to tell me soon." I finally say, gazing into his deep eyes before turning and walking away from him. My throat feels sore as the impending tears tempt the edges of my eyes. What is Matteo so afraid of? What is he so worried I'm going to find out about his mother?

CHAPTER 26

Daniela

I furiously work on the new dress design for the next week, and finish it just days before my deadline. While I hoped to take a large part in the launch of my new line, Rena ended up needing to go to multiple doctor visits and have even more monitoring than before. I don't mind taking care of her, of course, but this new launch was something I was looking forward to.

"We need to continue this little charade of ours," Ryan says. "I just haven't seen the reaction that I wanted."

"Ryan, I only agreed to do this until after the launch. This is going past what I agreed to." I argue.

"Daniela, you know, I wouldn't ask you this unless it was important for me," Ryan says, as though I'm supposed to feel sorry for him. "What about just two more outings? We agreed to that."

"Ryan, you know that I don't actually care about any of this, right?" I begin, feeling more frustrated with Ryan. "I'll do these last two outings, but then that's it. I don't want to be a part of this any longer, and I want you to expect that."

"I can agree to that, but I would like a little bit longer, if at all possible." He says, pushing his luck. "You have this insane popularity that I want to replicate."

"Ryan, why do you think I have this level of fame?" I say, reminding him that I'm only here because I'm self-made. "I built this myself, and you're never going to replicate what I have," I explain like I'm talking to a toddler.

"Yes, but that's not to say that all of the tabloids will not have an effect on the line I'm launching later this year," Ryan says, as though this makes everything better. "I have plans to make a big hit with this, and I think that with us being together around the time of your launch will really help that."

"Ryan, we're not together. Stop saying that. That's not what this is." Taking a breath, I continue. "It's nice that you're having your own launch, but again, I'm still not comfortable or happy with how this has been going."

"Yes, Daniela, but we had an agreement. It is an unusual agreement, but it was still an agreement, nonetheless. You agreed to help me, and that's what I expect you to do." Ryan says, sounding frustrated with my lack of interest in helping him. "And, I don't feel I've done anything to make you feel uncomfortable. Rather, you're uncomfortable with the idea of me becoming more famous than you." He says, completely missing the point of my speech.

"Ryan, you're just not getting it. I have a life, and you're ruining it. I don't want to be spending all this time with you, but here I am, going out and being photographed practically against my will, so you can steal my hard work. I understand wanting to have your designs seen all over the world, but you have to do it yourself. I did it, and so should you." I argue back, becoming more and more frustrated as our conversation continues.

"Yes, but you don't understand. I am on a strict deadline, and I need this fame now." Ryan says. "So, are we in agreement to meet tonight? We can go out somewhere in the city. I'll send you the location." He finishes.

"I guess so, but just know I'm becoming more and more frustrated. I don't want to be doing this anymore."

"Might I remind you, I'm not the one who jumped into your car." Why did I ever allow him to come into my house? I should have just told him to give me the jacket and find a restroom somewhere else. How did we spiral so far?

"Whatever, Ryan. Just message me the location, and I'll be there around seven." I say, trying to decide whether or not to let him speak before I hang up. Deciding on the latter, I press end call before he can get another word out.

"Do you see the photographer over there?" Ryan asks, gesturing to the discreetly placed photographer. "He's a photographer for most of the popular clothing news sites," Ryan says, his chest puffing with accomplishment.

"How wonderful," I say, taking a sip of water.

"Oh, at least act excited, Daniela," Ryan says, as though I should be thanking him.

"Be thankful that I'm doing something I don't want to

do?" I say lightly, so that to anyone else, it will seem like we're having a normal conversation.

"Thankful that this is even more of an opportunity to expand your business. Any news is good news, right?" Ryan says, as though he's the person who's being taken advantage of here.

"I don't think so, Ryan. How long do I have to be here?" I ask, glancing down at the watch on my wrist. I need to be home by nine, at least, because Reina needs help with her medication, and quite frankly, I don't want to be here with Ryan.

"Just stay an hour, I guess," Ryan says, sounding frustrated by my lack of excitement to be here with him. "I don't know why you're being so difficult, though."

"I'm not being difficult, Ryan. I'm really frustrated with how the events of this past month have gone, and I want out of this. I'm done pretending like this isn't a headache for me, and quite frankly, I shouldn't have to pretend that it isn't." I say, deciding on a small salad for dinner. I'm not hungry, but I know it will look strange if I don't have food.

Ryan always critiques my mannerisms around him, commenting that photographers will have a hard time finding good photos to use, and in all of them, I look less than happy, and I'm not actively engaging with him.

"Hello, what can I get for the lovely couple?" The waitress asks, approaching the table with a bright smile and her notepad.

"Oh, we aren't a couple. This is a business meeting." I say quickly, not even allowing Ryan to entertain the idea of this is as more than business.

"My bad, ma'am. We don't see many business meetings

here. My apologies." The waitress amends. I'm not mad with her, and I don't hold against her, but this is more for Ryan to remember that this is strictly a business agreement.

"I'd like the steak and lobster, please," Ryan says, looking over at me with a sharp intensity in his eyes. I'm sure it's because I quickly shut down the idea of us being a couple, but I don't really care.

"I'd love this salad, and would it be possible to add avocado and onion to it?" I ask, passing my menu to her as soon as she's done writing my order.

"Yes, of course. Let me get that for you." She says with a smile. "Have a lovely meeting."

CHAPTER 27

Daniela

Matteo meets my gaze as I enter The Enchanted Ivy, and the breath is stolen right out of my lungs. As though someone has sucked all of the oxygen from the room. His dark eyes search mine as I step towards him, and I'm not sure why I can't stop my body from moving towards him, but even if I could, I don't think I'd stop.

"You look beautiful tonight, Daniela," Matteo says, glancing me up and down before gazing into my eyes. He lifts his hand as if he's about to reach out to brush my hair with his fingertips, but instead of following along with the urge, he just drops it back to his side. "How is Lorena doing?" He asks, and I have to do a double-take. How did he know she isn't doing well?

"How did you know she's not doing well?" I ask. I haven't talked to him since the auction last week, and after that, Rena started going downhill again.

"Isn't that why you came back?" Matteo asks, as though he's also confused.

"Well, that's part of the reason I came back, but what I mean is, how do you know she's doing worse?" I ask, raising an eyebrow as his eyes widen.

"She's not improving?" Matteo seems to have genuine worry in his eyes, which doesn't necessarily surprise me, but it's also interesting. Of course, he spent time with her in high school, but not recently. "What's wrong with her?"

"She's not improving, and the doctors are quite concerned," I say, trying to sound as brave as possible. "I've been quite busy, trying to find the right doctors."

"If you need any help, please let me know," Matteo says quickly, as though this isn't even a question for him. It's just like him to try and save the day, but this seems like even more than that. Like he's genuinely worried and fears for Rena.

"Thank you, but I think that I found a good doctor yesterday. I wasn't able to participate as much as I would've liked to with my launch, but of course, Rena comes first." I say, finding it not at all difficult to be open and honest with him.

"I'm sorry to hear that. If it helps, Carmen has loved being a model for you, and it has really opened up a new path in her life. She's extremely excited to work with you again." Matteo says with a small smile.

"That makes me happy. I'm glad she found something she enjoys. She genuinely is good at this." I respond honestly, knowing it's the truth.

"Thank you. She's already amassed a whole bunch of followers on social media, and somehow, I became the manager of it all." Matteo says with a chuckle.

"How exciting. I bet you love that." I tease back. "Is being her manager everything you expected?" I continue, knowing that while it's totally out of his realm, he'd do anything for his siblings.

"Well, I wouldn't say it's everything I expected, but it's definitely very interesting. I had no idea what to expect when I decided to help her." He says. "Well, if we can even call it that. She came to me and said that I would be helping her, because she'd already asked our parents, with the stipulation that I would manage it all." Matteo says, his eyes twinkling.

"Oh, really? How often do you get suckered into things like this?" I say, referencing a time back in high school when I roped Matteo into helping me finish designing all of the costumes for one of the musicals our theater was putting on. Of course, the school had all the clothes made at some fancy manufacturing place, but the designs themselves were usually made by the students. I was the only one who signed up, and it was way too much work for one singular person, so I persuaded him to help me out.

"Yes, sometimes. Only for certain people, though." Matteo says, still joking, but something serious catches in his eyes.

"And who are those certain people?" I ask, still sounding like I'm teasing, but I do want to know. "What are the requirements?"

"Well, they're people who are very important to me," Matteo says, his Adam's apple bobbing as he speaks.

"Define important," I say, risking another gaze into his eyes. Maybe there's a part of me that wants to know if I was ever anything more than a high school love, and that's why I'm asking this.

"Well, someone that I think about regularly." He begins, speaking clearly. "Someone I would do anything for.

Someone I love." His eyes never leave mine as he says this. I'm not sure if it was intentional for him to say, love, instead of loved, but I pick up on it. I'm about to ask him for a deeper explanation, but the dinner host is starting to signal that it's time to be seated.

Matteo sits near his family, where his seat card is, and I am further down the table with groups of two or three people, not whole families.

Glancing down at Matteo one last time, he meets my eyes, as though he can hear my thoughts. "Meet me outside later?" He mouths, and I nod my head, but quickly turn my attention back to the conversation surrounding me. Of course, nothing we're doing isn't allowed, but I'd still feel strange if people were watching us.

Conversation flows around me, and I try to interact, but my mind is racing a hundred miles a minute. I'm not sure what Matteo is going to tell me outside, but the thought of being with him is enough to send my brain into a frenzy.

Once I'm done with this stupid plan of Ryan's, I should be able to maintain a relationship with Matteo. Sure, Rena's health is a problem, but it shouldn't be something difficult to manage alongside a relationship. I just hope that when we're able to try and make things work, we're not unfixable.

When everybody starts leaving, I almost don't notice Matteo standing, until he brushes by my chair, his fingers gently tracing the skin on my shoulders and back of my neck as he walks. It sends shivers throughout my body, and I try to keep a composed expression as I give him time to exit, without it, making it seem as though we're leaving together.

With the memory of Matteo's touch burned in my mind, I stand and smooth my dress as I follow the direction he left in. There are multiple entries and exits to The Enchanted Ivy, and it appears as though he went out one of the glass doors to the side. I spot him near the tennis court as I stride down the path.

I was never as good at tennis as Matteo was, but I enjoyed playing with him nonetheless, back in high school. It was fun to watch him do something he enjoyed, and simply have the entertainment of joining him.

"Are you challenging me to a match?" I tease, lifting my dress slightly as I walk towards him. The grass isn't deep by any means, but the fringe of my dress is white, and I don't feel like having to work out grass stains later.

"Would you like to?" Matteo asks, as though this wasn't a thought in his mind before. "I didn't bring you out here with the intention of playing tennis, but by all means, if you'd like to, I will. Although, you need to watch out, because I haven't practiced in years, and I'm sure my aim will definitely be off." Matteo says bashfully.

"Why did you stop playing?" I ask, intrigued by the idea of him dropping his favorite sport.

"After we broke up, the idea of playing with someone other than you wasn't appealing." He admits, as though he's not admitting to quitting his favorite sport, all because we broke up.

"Oh, I didn't realize that. Well, it's been just as long since I've played, and we already know that I'm the poor player out of the two of us." I say, trying to lighten the mood. I remind myself that he's the one who broke up with me, but the thought of years going by without him playing tennis brings a pang of sadness to me.

"I'm sure you're not that bad, Daniela," Matteo says,

looking down at my red dress before glancing back up. "Are you sure you want to do this in a dress?" He asks.

"Are you saying I can't do it in a dress?" I tease, looking up through my eyelashes. "If so, I accept your challenge, Mr. Alvarez," I say, stepping past him and onto the court. I have no idea why I'm doing this, or why I'm even entertaining the idea of playing tennis in a dress, but the thought of doing anything with Matteo, even in a dinner dress, is appealing.

"As you wish, Miss Lozano," Matteo says, stepping after me and reaching out to pick up the hem of my dress as it drags down the court. He carries it lightly in his hand, and although it's not even above my knees, it feels like such an intimate gesture.

Matteo grabs two rackets and a ball, and I have to admit that this might be one of my funniest, 'do it for the plot' moments. I mean, who else wears a formal dress while they play tennis? At least the court we're in is far away from the main building, and there's no one else out here. Only Matteo to witness me helplessly swing the racket at the ball.

This has always been Matteo's thing, and I've always been happy to humor him and play along as best as possible. Just like how Matteo would spend hours with me in my living room with paper after paper of clothing designs.

"Are you sure you don't want to put this dress with that collection?" Matteo asks from his spot on the floor across from me. "Don't you think it will go well with that tuxedo and those shoes?"

"Hey, you're right! This might be exactly what I need!" I exclaim, reaching over to take the paper from him as I set it in the line of clothing I've been organizing for the past week. While I still have months until I can actually open a business, I need to have everything else ready.

"Now, who said I'm not good with fashion?" Matteo teases, reaching over to poke my ribs. I squirm away, squealing in protest.

"Hey!" I laugh, falling back onto the floor.

Matteo follows, still tickling my shoulder as he flops down next to me, his shoulder pressed against mine. "I told you I can help you." He says proudly, turning his head to face mine. "You know that I want to be here for you, no matter what, right?"

"Yeah, I know," I reply, pushing off the floor so that I can rest my head on his shoulder. "I guess I was wrong when I said you were being unhelpful."

"I know people are going to love your designs, Daniela," Matteo says, softly brushing a kiss to my forehead, sending a million butterflies fluttering in my stomach.

"Matteo, I'm only seventeen. Who will take an eighteen-year-old seriously in a few months?" I fret, lifting my eyes to study his jaw before he answers.

"They'll take you seriously, Daniela. Your age won't matter when everyone sees the talent and hard work you've put into your designs and plans. If no one else will watch you, then I'll always be here. You'll always have a supporter in me." Matteo says softly as he wraps his arm around my waist. His voice is low, and hearing the rumble of it on his chest helps remove some of the worry from my body.

"Thank you," I reply, closing my eyes. The easy breaths

that rise his chest are like a lullaby, and all of the pent-up stress evaporates the longer he holds me.

"Ready?" Matteo calls out, pulling me from the memory that took place just two weeks before my world turned upside down.

"Yep," I call back, just barely whacking the tennis ball as it comes across the net. Matteo is surely taking it easy on me, and while I hardly ever appreciate being intentionally taken easy on, this is the one time I'm thankful. This has always been his thing.

"That was really good!" He says, gently tapping the ball back to me.

"Thank you," I reply, already feeling the stamina leaving my muscles as we play. It's already rather dark outside, and only a singular light is on out here. Alone.

Playing—if you can even call it that—is keeping all of my attention, and I'm grateful when Matteo suggests taking a break. The air has grown considerably colder, and as I make a jump at deflecting the ball, I land wrong on my heel, and my ankle twists with a sharp pain. "Ouch!" I yelp, immediately dropping my racket as I reach down to remove my shoe to assess the damage.

"Daniela? Are you okay?" Matteo calls, completely forgetting the game as he rushes over to me and drops to his knees at my feet as he also glances over my ankle.

"Yeah, I think I'm okay. It's just really sore." I reply, the sharp pain dulling to a throb.

"Let's take a break, Daniela. I should have realized that you weren't in the appropriate attire for playing tennis, and definitely shouldn't have hit that ball so hard." Matteo apologizes. He takes the racket from my hands and places it with the ball and the other racket on the designated shelf near the edge of the court. "Thank you for playing with me. I guess I didn't realize how much I missed it." He says as he approaches me. "I'm still very sorry for your ankle, though. Hopefully, it's not seriously injured. Do you think we need to go to the doctor?"

"Oh, come on, Matteo. It's nothing more than a simple misstep. It'll be better by morning." I reply easily as I take a step forward. Ouch. That still really hurts. "I merely just swung the racket around in hopes of hitting the ball. I hardly qualify that as playing." Trying to conceal my wince, I lean against him lightly while we walk.

"No, I really had a nice time. Even if your swing was a little rusty." Matteo teases back. "I'm totally joking, though. I'm just happy you're here and wanted to play." He quickly adds, looking down to meet my eyes as though he needs to know he was only joking.

"Relax, Matteo. I know I'm pretty terrible at tennis. I also know that you're only joking." I answer, glancing up through my eyelashes as I speak.

"Would you like to sit?" Matteo asks, gesturing down at the couches and chairs that glow in the twinkle of the fairy lights that surround the outdoor lounge.

After we're comfortably seated, I glance at the space in between us and imagine moving just a little bit closer to him. Would he move away? Move closer? Wrap his arm around my shoulder? As these questions swirl around in my mind, I notice Matteo watching me closely, as though he's wondering the same thing as I am.

"What did you do while I was away at college?" I question, suddenly needing to know how he kept himself busy.

"Well, I graduated from college in two years, I work for my father's company, and-" He breaks off at the end of his sentence, as though there's something that's keeping him from talking about the rest of it.

"And?" I press, my eyes teasing as he chews his lip.

"Well, I also bought a house on the outskirts of the city, but it's not fully remodeled yet." He finishes quickly.

"Really? That's pretty amazing." I comment. Matteo is a homeowner? Sure, it's natural for people to grow up and move out, but Matteo growing up and moving out?

There are two sides of my brain, and while one knows that Matteo is twenty-one years old and an adult, the other still imagines him as the seventeen-year-old who couldn't see a future past college.

"Thank you. It's been a difficult four years, but I think it's been good for me to busy myself with things that will further my future." Matteo says honestly, his eyes conveying something that his mouth won't.

"Why have these four years been hard?" I ask, taking a deep breath once the question has left my body.

"Daniela, I don't think you know just how much I've missed you." Matteo begins. He pauses, as though he's not going to finish his speech, but he seems to press himself to finish. "Life has been dull without you. It felt like I was living in a world without color. I know that I'm the one who broke up with you, but I've regretted it every second of every day."

For a moment, I'm unable to formulate a single word. While I felt somewhat the same way, I think the grief of losing my parents at the same time overshadowed the grief of losing my relationship, and as I worked through it all, I healed the part of me that grieved a relationship with Matteo. That's not to say I don't want a relationship with him—quite the opposite—but rather, I think that instead of needing him like I used to, I want him.

"That's..." I search for the right thing to say, but still come up with nothing. "I'm sorry you've struggled these last few years, Matteo. You're doing better now, though?" For some reason, the shock of his confession is leaving me at a loss for words.

"Now that you're here, I'm better," Matteo answers, his Adam's apple bobbing as he speaks. "That was the biggest mistake of my life, and I never want to repeat it again. I've never forgiven myself for that, and I don't think I ever will. I hurt you when you were already hurting, and it was the wrong thing to do."

Tears prickle at the edges of my eyes as the memories of being seventeen flood back. My parents passing unexpectedly, and losing the only boy I'd ever loved two weeks later, was the worst time in my life. I always try to skip over those memories when I recall high school, since breaking down over the unfairness of life is pointless, but there are always a few moments when I can't help but remember the deep, sharp pain that followed me around like my own personal storm cloud.

"Why did you break up with me?" I venture, knowing

that he's probably going to be untruthful once again. Which might be warranted, since I'm not exactly being honest about Ryan, either.

Matteo must see the emotion behind my eyes, because he immediately sobers any of his raw emotions and immediately kicks into protective mode. "I can't tell you right now, but maybe when we have more time to sit down and talk about it, I might be able to explain it all." Matteo finally says, as though this is against his better judgment, but he knows that I won't take no for an answer.

"Why not right now?" I question, leaning slightly closer to him. "What are you hiding from me?"

"Something that will break your heart." He admits, swallowing loud enough that I can hear it. "Something that I never should have agreed to."

My heart thuds at his admittance that whatever he's keeping from me is bad, and I chew my lower lip as I consider this. How bad is it? Is it something that will do more harm than good to know about?

"How bad is it?" I whisper, a million thoughts rushing around my mind. "What did you do?" My breaths come in quick, shallow movements as the tension between us increases. Matteo glances around us as though he wishes he could be anywhere but here.

"I didn't do anything except for-" He breaks off and clears his throat before continuing. "I wasn't lying when I said that my parents are the reason we broke up."

My heart slows ever so slightly at the confirmation that it really was his parents forcing him to break up with me. Sure, I might have thought about him dating someone else after me, but when he said that it would break my heart, the worst possible situation came to mind. I've never thought of Matteo as a cheater, and I don't think that anything on this earth would bring him to cheat on me, or any other woman, for that matter.

"Well, that's comforting," I say a little bit softer now. "Then why did they make you break up with me?"

"Daniela, I can't tell you right now. We can talk about it when you're not already vulnerable like this." Matteo says firmly, further solidifying the idea that whatever this is about is something terrible. "I have to look out for you, and telling you right now isn't the right thing to do. Initially, I wasn't ever going to tell you why, but I know you deserve the truth. Right now, just isn't the right time to tell you, though."

"But you're going to tell me?" I press. Something in my heart won't allow me to fully open up to Matteo again unless he's going to tell me the truth, and I think Matteo knows it, too. It's not fair of him to assume that it won't matter to me, but I don't necessarily think that he assumes that. I genuinely believe that he thinks he's protecting me from the truth.

"Yes, I will," Matteo says, sounding more and more confident in his answer now.

"Thank you, Matteo." I finally say, suddenly noticing the darkness around us. What time is it? Matteo seems to notice my sudden awareness for the time, and checks his watch.

"It's midnight, Daniela." He says gently, before a teasing light appears in his eyes. "Don't tell me that you're about to disappear at the last strike of twelve."

"I don't know, maybe I am," I tease, standing up to

jokingly walk away. Yikes. Big mistake. "Ow, ow, ow!" I yelp, falling immediately back onto the sofa.

"Are you okay? What's wrong?" Matteo asks, jumping up from his end of the chair to stand in front of me. I glance down, and the swelling on my ankle has only increased since earlier. The adrenaline must have dulled the pain when I walked then. Now, the sharp spikes of pain make it almost impossible to walk.

"I think my ankle is still really sore," I admit. The furrow between Matteo's eyebrows deepens as his worry increases.

"Let's get you to a doctor, then." He says almost immediately, as though he regularly goes to the doctor's office for a twisted ankle.

"No, no. I'm sure it just needs some ice and elevation." I protest, knowing that this really will be better by morning.

"Daniela, are you sure? If you need the doctor, please tell me." Matteo replies, sinking to his ankles as he gently brushes my dress and the straps of my shoe aside, so he can really inspect the swelling. My skin reacts immediately to his touch, and a small cluster of goosebumps floods the area of my ankle.

"I really think it will be okay in the morning. It's just a little bit sore right now." I say reassuringly. My breath hitches as his fingers graze the area around the clasp, as if he's deciding whether or not to remove the shoe altogether.

"I'm going to take these off for you, okay?" Matteo says, slowly unbuckling the shoe on my left foot, before moving to my right. For a moment, I don't say anything, because the sight of him on his knees in front of me, inspecting my injury, while taking off my shoes, is too much to handle.

"But how am I going to walk?" I question, my mind fuzzy as I speak.

"You're not going to." He replies easily, standing with both of my shoes and my small leather purse in his hand, all hanging by the straps. I don't have any time to process what's happening, until suddenly I'm in Matteo's strong, safe arms. He's carrying me bridal style, all while my shoes are still dangling from his fingers that are at my knees.

"Matteo, I don't think you'll be able to carry me all of the way back to the car," I say, imagining the mile-long walk back to my car.

"Are you doubting my knight in shining armor abilities?" Matteo teases with a scoff as he effortlessly lifts me even tighter, pulling me impossibly closer to his chest.

"I guess not," I finally admit, snuggling into him as he saunters down the path.

"Good," Matteo replies, and I can almost hear the smirk in his voice.

"Hey, Matteo, why did you want to talk to me earlier today? When you asked me to meet you outside, what were you going to tell me?" I ask, suddenly realizing that we never got to the point of why we were out here.

"I honestly don't remember," Matteo says, as though really considering my question. "Seeing you unnerved by the people around you made me want to do something, and the first thing I could think of was to get you out of that situation."

"Really?" My voice is softer now, and it must have something to do with how safe I feel in Matteo's arms.

"Really." Matteo says. His breath and voice haven't changed one bit since he started carrying me, and while I don't particularly think that I'm extremely heavy, it's definitely comforting the part of me that was worried about him walking the whole mile back to my car.

The gentle rustle of trees and the sound of chirping crickets fill our silence, and I want to stay here forever.

"Thank you," I say as we reach my car. "You walked so fast," I comment as I realize how quickly the walk from the tennis court to my car was.

"Anytime, Daniela," Matteo says easily, moving all of my weight to his right arm, using his left—which is still holding my shoes and purse—to reach into my bag and pull out my car keys. The car lights flicker, and Matteo opens the driver's door. "Will you be able to drive home?"

"Matteo, I just need to ice and elevate it," I say, throwing my head back as I laugh. "It hurts, but this isn't life-threatening by any means. Just a twisted ankle."

"If you're sure that you're able to, then here," Matteo says easily, leaning down to place me in the driver's seat. "Oh, here are your shoes and purse." He quickly adds, extending the items to me.

"Thank you for everything," I say, gesturing at the shoes I just placed on the floorboard, then to my purse, and finally, my ankle. "You really saved me from having to walk all of the way back with a sore ankle."

"You were injured because you were playing tennis with me, so that was my fault." Matteo chuckles, leaning against the frame of my car. If I already didn't think he's tall, sitting in a car while he stands outside would make it extremely apparent.

"Maybe, but the whole tennis idea was entirely mine, so I have to take accountability there," I say before chuckling along with him. "It appears I'm very rusty." I motion to my foot, and even though it's only dimly lit from the car lights, Matteo still peers at it once more, as though to assure himself that it's nothing more than a twisted ankle.

"Well, I'm right there with you. I haven't played in just as long. I'm surprised I didn't sprain my wrist or something." He says easily, as though our skills have always been evenly matched.

"Be quiet, Matteo," I say with a roll of my eyes as I reach up to slap his chest. Only, since I'm much lower than I usually am, my hand only reaches his stomach. Well, if he has a stomach under his rock-hard abs. Quickly, I remove my hand, but not before I meet Matteo's smirk.

"As you wish, ma'am," Matteo says, moving his hand in what looks like a gesture of zipping his lips and throwing away the key.

I don't want this moment between us to end, but it's already twelve-thirty. Rena has already received all of her evening stuff, but she might still be awake waiting for me.

"I should probably get home," I finally say with a sigh after a few moments of peaceful silence between us.

"I had a nice time with you, Daniela. Let's do it again sometime. Especially since your launch is over." Matteo says, only slightly pointedly. Right. I told him that after my launch, I would have time for us, but now with Ryan still around, and Rena needing even more care, it doesn't feel like even slightly calmer.

"Yeah, I'd like that." I can't keep avoiding Matteo, and I don't want to, either. I want him.

CHAPTER 28

Matteo

The meeting between Father and Mr. Valentino is rather uneventful—as expected—and while the meeting progresses, I can't help my mind from wandering. I'm not worried about Mr. Valentino doing something outrageous, since he and Father are more or less friends, and they've worked everything out beforehand.

Daniela pops back into mind, and the memory of her hair bouncing behind her as she whacked the balls back at me—before she twisted her ankle—replays over and over. Maybe it's stupid, but we felt like "us" again two nights ago. Laughing, joking, having deep conversations, everything reminded me of when we were in high school.

It's not that I want our high school relationship back, because obviously, we're older and grown, but I want the simplicity of us back.

The vibrating of my phone on the chair next to me breaks through my train of thought—or, lack thereof—and

I quickly glance over to make sure it didn't interrupt the conversation a few feet down from me.

Santiago is actually paying attention for once, and I can't help but suspect that there's a girl in his life right now. Not just any girl, but someone who's making him want to be more. Within the past few weeks, there's been a complete shift in him, and he's been even more secretive than usual.

My phone buzzes again, and I discreetly lift it to check the caller identification.

Daniela.

Why is she calling me? Last I knew, I was blocked from her contact list. Quickly pressing accept call, I stand and rush out of the room, only giving Santiago a quick glance before closing the door behind me.

"Hello?"

"Matteo, I know this is kind of strange, and totally a disruption to your day, but I need you."

"What's wrong?"

"Rena just started going downhill health-wise again, so I took her to the doctor, and they're going to have her here overnight as they give her a new medication, since they need to rule out the allergic reaction risk." Daniela begins, taking a deep breath before continuing. "So, she's fine now, since they think this is going to help with the interior healing, but I can't leave her here to get the stuff we need to spend the night."

"Just text me a list and your location, and I'll have it all for you by-" I check my watch and calculate the time from when I can leave in ten minutes, to how long it will take to gather a list of stuff. "-four."

"Thank you so much. I'll text you all of the stuff in a few minutes."

"Don't worry about it, Daniela," I say gently, leaning against the hallway walls as I speak. "I'm happy to do this for you."

"Thank you, Matteo. I'll see you later."

On my drive to Lorena's house, Daniela texts me the list of things she needs. Once I've parked in the driveway, I reach into one of the many flowerpots on the porch, pulling out a spare key to the house.

It's been over two months since I've had to use the key, so I'm a little surprised to find that it's still here, right where Lorena left it.

Daniela's list specifies blankets from the closet, a few pillows, her computer, the charger, and a bag that seems to enclose all of the other medication.

It doesn't take very long, and in fifteen minutes, I'm back on the road towards the doctor's office. The drive feels like forever, and my thoughts race as I consider the afternoon. I don't know if I just assumed that Daniela would leave me blocked on her phone forever, but the surprise of the caller identification was quickly shoved to the back of my mind as she spoke about needing my help.

"Excuse me, who are you here to see?" The receptionist in the lobby asks as I approach her.

"Lorena Arango." I say easily, pulling out my identification, so she can add me to the system.

"Thank you. I do have a note here that the caregiver of the patient has approved you for a visitation." The receptionist replies, passing me back my identification, and a small key card that will allow me entrance to the room.

"Thank you."

I knock on the door to Lorena's room, instead of using the key card, since it seems rather rude to barge into the room when I know Daniela is able to answer.

"Matteo? Is that you?" I hear Daniela's voice as she approaches the door. "Oh my gosh, thank you so much." She says, motioning for me to follow her into the room. "Rena, look who is here to visit us."

"Matteo, thank you so much for coming," Lorena says somewhat excitedly from her bed. "How did Daniela convince you to come?"

"She said that you needed help, and of course, I was on my way," I say, my eyes meeting Daniela's as I speak.

We talk for a few more moments, but Lorena quickly falls asleep, and Daniela and I make ourselves comfortable on the couch near the window.

"Thank you so much, Matteo," Daniela says, reaching over to clasp her hand over mine. "The doctor said that we should see a significant improvement with the medicine, and we should be out of here by morning. Until then, I'm just going to be hanging out and praying for smooth sailing."

"I'll stay here with you," I say, glancing around the room, as though these are my new quarters. "Of course, you don't need to let me stay," I add, meaning it.

"You don't have to do that, Matteo," Daniela says quickly, as though she thinks this will be a burden to me. "It will be rather boring, and I don't think there's much to do."

"That's not a problem. I'm just here to support you. And, Lorena, of course." I say, rubbing my thumb along the length of her finger.

"If you have nothing else to do, I would love your company." She says with a smile, her hair bouncing as she nods her head.

Hours pass by, with hundreds of rounds of Go Fish and various other card games played by us. We're silent sometimes, and other times, we fill the space between us with conversation. None of it is rather interesting, as though we're both dancing around the elephant in the room. Our current relationship.

"It's just like old times," Lorena says softly from her bed, sounding barely awake. Daniela jumps up, dropping her cards in the process, as she strides to the bed.

"What do you mean, Rena?" She asks, reaching down to brush a singular strand of hair from her forehead.

"I mean, that's just like when your boy would bring me the things I needed." She says softly, closing her eyes again, and falling back into a soft slumber.

"Sorry, I don't know what she's talking about. The doctor said that this medication will make her sleepy for a few hours, but I guess it also makes her delirious?" Lorena was never supposed to mention anything to Daniela, but I guess I can't be upset with her, because she is in the doctor's office on medicine. "Do you know what she's talking about?" Daniela asks, suddenly very interested in what I have to say.

"Well, I brought her groceries here and there, so that's probably what she's referencing," I say as casually as possible. Lorena was never supposed to tell Daniela that I helped her with shopping, making appointments, yard work, and so on.

"You bought her groceries?" Daniela asks, sounding more than confused. "When?"

"Oh, just whenever she needed something. I had a lot of extra time on my hands, and it was really no inconvenience to help her out." I say, trying to dismiss the whole conversation. Daniela, on the other hand, doesn't seem so ready to drop it.

"How long has this been going on for? When did you start it?" Daniela presses, peering even deeper into my eyes.

"Well, I think it was a week after you left for college, and I was in town, and wanted to drop by the grocery store—which, I don't do very often—and I happened to run into Lorena. She was struggling to get something off the top shelf, so I helped her, and then ended up helping her get the rest of her list. After that, I helped her take it home, unload it, and told her to call me if she ever needed anything." I say, taking a breath as I think back all of those years ago. "A week or two later, she called me, saying that she was struggling to get one of her plants moved across the porch, and wanted to know if I could help her. Of course, I said, yes, and after that, she called me whenever she needed help, whenever she needed groceries, or needed to be driven somewhere."

"Wow, I had no idea," Daniela says, swallowing deeply as she considers everything said. "Thank you for looking after her. When I left, I didn't think about how vulnerable I would be leaving Rena, and I'm glad you were here to take care of her," she says, me, and my guys once again.

"It was really no problem, and I enjoyed spending so much time with her. Since you've been back, I haven't wanted to intrude, so it's been strange to not see her so often." I say, chuckling lightly.

"Wait, were you the one who took her to the doctor initially? When she fell?" Daniela suddenly asks, as if this thought hadn't come to her mind before now. "Because I didn't think about her getting to the doctor's office, but surely she was driven, right?"

I rub the back of my neck, suddenly feeling like this question is very important to Daniela. "Yes, that was me. She called me to come over and help move some boxes downstairs, since she wanted to clean out her upper level, and I was on my way, when she must have fallen. When she didn't answer as I knocked, I used the spare key to come in and saw her on the floor." The memory hurts me, as I remember my mind immediately jumping to the worst-case scenario.

Daniela's hand flies to her mouth as she considers just how terrible that would've been. "I can't thank you enough, Matteo. Really, it was selfish of me to leave Rena all by herself, but you really stepped in and helped. I can't imagine what would've happened, had you not already been on your way over." Daniela says, before pressing her lips together. "Is that how you got in the house earlier? The spare key?"

"Yes. I assumed it was still there, and it was a second nature for me to use it." I reply, leaning back in my chair, since apparently, this interrogation will be lasting much longer.

"Wow, so I guess it wasn't difficult for you to get the blankets and everything, because you must've spent a lot of time at her house." She comments.

"You could say that," I tease, trying to make light of the

situation. "You know she'll get better, right?" I finally say, answering the concern that's been dancing in Daniela's eyes all afternoon.

"What?"

"Lorena will be fine. The doctors will heal her, and she'll be out of here by morning." I say, reaching over to brush a few stray hairs out of Daniela's face.

"So, it appears you can still read my mind." Is all Daniela says, leaning into my touch at her cheek. The feeling of her skin on mine is unexpected, but I'm grateful for it.

"Or, I just know the facts. Lorena is strong, and this new medicine will help her. You don't need to worry." I say, knowing that this is very difficult for her. After losing her parents, Lorena is her last living relevant relative.

"I know she's strong, but that still doesn't change the fact that I worry for her. She's not as young as she used to be, and she's the only person I have left." Daniela says softly, as though this has been weighing on her for a while. "There's no one else here for me, and if I lose Rena, I'll be fully alone."

"You're not going to lose her, Daniela." I start, gazing intently into her eyes. "And, you have me. No matter what's happening between us, I still care for you so much, and I'll always be here for you." I say, finally moving my hand away from her face. I don't want to, but I know that I have to.

"But I did lose you, Matteo," Daniela says softly, reminding me that I broke up with her. I suck in the breath, knowing that she's right.

"Even though I broke up with you, I never stopped loving you. I never stop caring for you. And I definitely never stopped wishing that I could go back in time and stop myself from destroying you like that." I say, gently, trying to put as much sincerity as possible in my voice.

"Do you really mean that?" Daniela questions, as though there's still doubt about how I feel for her. That's my fault, though. A normal person doesn't break up with someone that they claim to love.

"Daniela, if I could go back in time, I would never have broken up with you. I would have done things so very differently, and I promise that I never in a million years wanted to hurt you."

"Then why did you do it?" Daniela asks, her voice firmer now. "You need to tell me why you broke up with me. I deserve to know, and you told me the other night that you would tell me." I can't say no to her. Not anymore.

"It's really going to hurt you, and I'd understand if you hated me forever," I begin, noting how Daniela's eyes widen. "It was my parents who made me break up with you."

"Oh, yeah. Why, though? Why were you worried about what your mother said to me the other day?" Daniela asks, already taking this better than I expected.

"Well, this is where it's the really bad part," I say, my throat suddenly feeling extremely tight. The room is too hot, the lights are too bright, and Daniela's expression is too expectant for someone who's about to have her heart crushed.

"Go on, Matteo." She encourages, her gaze unwavering from mine.

"They said that since your parents had passed, you'd now be a lower-class level without them." My throat burns as I admit this. Daniela's jaw drops, and tears immediately start streaming down her cheeks.

"And you agreed with them?" She practically shouts, before realizing where we are. Lorena is still asleep, and these walls can't be that thick.

"No, of course not," I rush out, realizing I should have said that part first. "But they threatened to disown and kick me out if I continued dating you. You know how much I wanted to please them, back then. When they threatened to cut me off, I was absolutely terrified and did what they told me to do. Which was breaking up with you. I'm so sorry."

Daniela is still crying, but she does appear to be listening, which is at least a positive. My heart twists and knots at the pain I know I've brought upon her, and again, the wish to go back in time and change it all washes over me.

"So, you agreed to break up with me because you didn't want your parents to disown you? And it wasn't because you were worried about being seen with the girl who just lost her parents?" Daniela questions. I debate reaching out to brush the tears that are flowing down her cheeks, wondering if she even wants me to touch her, but I can't help myself.

"Of course. For the record, if I could do it again, I would never break up with you, and I would face their wrath a billion times over before losing you. I now know that nothing will ever come before you again, and I'm so, so sorry it took me losing you to realize that." I say, reaching out to brush the pad of my thumb against her cheek. Daniela moves her face back, and the pain of knowing that I've brought so much harm to her tears my heart apart.

"Matteo, I need space from you right now. Thank you for being honest with me, but I need space to think about this and process my emotions." Daniela says, standing from her chair, signaling that this conversation is over.

"I understand," I say, standing in front of her now. For just a second, I don't see the confident and strong version of the woman Daniela is today. Instead, I'm instantly transported back to right before I broke up with her. When Daniela's life was so upside down, and all that was left of her was a broken shell of the outgoing girl she used to be.

"I just need space from you, right now. With Rena being where she is health-wise, I need to focus on her. I'm not mad at you for telling me, and I don't think I blame you for doing what you did, but I just need space right now." Daniela says as I exit the door. Risking one glance back at her, there are fresh tears welling at the corners of her eyes, and it's all I can do not to turn around and continue apologizing.

CHAPTER 29

Daniela

"Daniela, did your boy leave?" Rena calls from her bed. Immediately, I rush over to her and take her hand in mine.

"Yes, he did, but don't worry about it. How are you feeling? They said you might be tired after all of the medication started working." I say, gently brushing a few strays of her hair off her face.

"Oh, dear, I feel just fine. What I want to worry about is why that boy of yours isn't here." Rena insists, covering my hand with hers.

"He told me why he broke up with me, and I needed to be alone while I processed all of it." I finally say.

"Well, you've had time alone, right? When are you going to talk to him?" Rena questions, as though this is the obvious response.

"You're not even curious about why he broke up with me?" I ask. This is not the Rena I know. She needs each and every detail about anything.

"I already know why he broke up with you, Daniela,"

Rena says simply, like it's common knowledge, and I'm the only person who didn't know.

"What? How?"

"He told me." Rena replies easily.

"Just like he helped you out regularly?" I ask suspiciously. Maybe it's just the day I've had, but something about Rena not telling me she spent so much time with Matteo rubs me the wrong way. "He told me all about that, by the way."

"Daniela, if I had told you, you would've avoided coming home. Besides, the boy needed someone in his life to help guide him." Rena says easily.

"What do you mean? I wouldn't have avoided coming home." I huff, knowing that she's completely right. I was terrified of the idea of seeing Matteo again. From the mixed emotions because of our breakup, to not knowing what I wanted from him, I would have one hundred percent avoided visiting home, had I had the inkling of a suspicion that I would see him at Rena's house.

"Daniela, you were both so lost in life, and the only thing I could do was support you. He needed it just as much as you did." Rena continues, meeting my gaze with more passion than I've seen in a long time. "Your boy was struggling with everything going on in his life, and he genuinely hated himself for breaking up with you. Not only because it hurt him, but mostly because it hurt you. He loves you so very much, my dear. More than you'll ever know."

More tears spring to my eyes, and I don't even fight them when they begin running down my cheeks. "I know he loves me, Rena. I'm just struggling with so much and don't want to ruin us before we even have a real chance at forever."

"Daniela, you've only scratched the surface of how much he loves you. The way he speaks about you is of a man in love. He's seen into the deepest and darkest parts of you and shines his light there. You do the same for him. I'm not saying that you have to do anything, but if I were you, I would give Matteo a second chance." Rena says, her voice a little bit softer now as her strength wanes.

"You really think so?"

"I know so, Daniela. He is hopelessly and extraordinarily in love with you. You'll never find a man who loves you more than him. That's not to say that there aren't other men out there, but he knows you, Daniela. He knows everything that should scare him away, and he embraces it with love."

CHAPTER 30

Daniela

"Yes, just make sure you keep an eye on her, and no overly stressful situations, of course." The nurse says as Rena and I walk out of the room.

We've been discharged, and the doctors really think that this new medication will work. After just under twenty-four hours spent in the hospital, maybe, just maybe, this will be a fresh start for everything. For Rena and her health, and for Matteo and I.

"Are you ready to get home?" I ask Rena as I pull out of the parking lot. Her smile is infectious, and I can't help but mirror it.

"Being in there was too stuffy and harsh. You know I need my soft light and colors. Oh, and my open windows, too." Rena huffs, as though we could have just skipped the whole overnight stay.

"Yes, I do. I'm glad we're going home. How about I make us some soup, and we watch one of your telenovelas?" I offer. There's no way I'll be able to be productive after these last twenty-four hours, so I might as well make the best out of it and spend time with Rena.

"Ryan, I told you that I spent all of yesterday and this morning in the hospital with my grandmother. It's crazy to me that you don't seem to have an ounce of sympathy for someone who's going through all of this." I hiss, taking the steps two at a time. I definitely don't need Rena to hear this conversation.

"Yes, but we had an agreement," Ryan complains, his voice grating on my nerves.

"That's the unfortunate thing about shady agreements. Either party can fall through at any moment." I say, the pent-up frustration with this whole situation starting to overflow the longer we talk.

"Fine, fine. How does four days from now sound?" Ryan finally says. He's starting to realize that I don't have any plans of making this easy for him, and his only option is to just work around my schedule.

"That actually doesn't work. I have an appointment that evening, so pick another day. Choose wisely, because this is the last time I'm doing anything with you again." I warn, the idea of being free of Ryan and his ridiculous schemes tantalizing.

"Daniela, this is really a struggle to work around your schedule, you know?" Ryan complains, and there's a shuffling on the other end of the line that sounds like Ryan going through his schedule. "Fine. A week from now. Does that work?"

"Yes, I can make that work. After that, I won't be hearing from you ever again." I reply, leaning my hip against the kitchen counter as I survey the grocery list I need to order today.

"Yes, yes. Anyway, I'll see you in a week." Ryan says before ending the call. Ugh. How am I going to deal with him for another week? Sighing, I pull my hair back into a clip that barely restrains a third of my hair.

I know what my options are. Yes, I have lawyers, but there's no way that we'll win any kind of case against a whole family of lawyers. Heck, there's probably at least ten judges in his family. This is even less about the fact that I can't go through with a legal battle, but more about we'll never win. Besides, that level of stress will be terrible for Rena's health. No stress is crucial for her health.

CHAPTER 31

Matteo

"Matteo, do you know what's going on with your brother? Apparently, he decided to hop on a plane with that actress and show up to the premiere of her movie." Mother says, brushing her hands against her dress as she reaches for her clutch. Quite frankly, I've been wondering the same thing. Santiago has been known for his rash ideas, but jetting off to New York City with Brooklynn Carmine is his most extravagant one yet.

"No, I don't. Haven't you talked to him?" I say, running a hand through my hair at her mini-interrogation.

"No, we haven't, but we figured you might know something. We just haven't been able to get him to open up, and it appears that at this point, he's willing to do whatever he feels like, without any second thought to what we feel is best." Mother says, sounding both frustrated, and maybe, just a little bit hurt. My parents have never been known for prioritizing a relationship with their children, but it almost seems that Mother is sad about it.

Mentally, I make a note to talk to him tonight, because I do miss him. Not knowing what he was doing or where he was, and then seeing him looking the happiest he's ever been at the premiere of a movie with a girl he just met, was quite the wake-up call. Sure, I've tried recently to rekindle our friendship, but seeing how I knew so little of his life, to the point that I was unaware of the fact that he was going to be in New York, on the red-carpet premiere of his girlfriend's movie, was quite the slap in the face.

Not to even mention, I didn't even know he had a girlfriend. The only thing I can say is that he must really love her. His smile was one that I haven't seen in years, and she looked just as happy. There was a light in his eyes that has never appeared more than once or twice in his whole life.

As for Carmen, I'm not even sure what to do anymore. The other day, just a few hours after I was helping Daniela at the hospital, we were at The Enchanted Ivy, and I guess something happened between Carmen and the guy, Emilio, and Santiago got in a fight with him. Well, during that, Carmen ended up telling Santiago that she was dating his ex-best friend, Alessandro Valentino.

If I ever thought that I was failing as a brother before, that version of myself would hate to see me now. How did both of my siblings go from being close with me, to both of them dating, without telling anybody?

Carmen just felt like announcing her boyfriend right after Santiago and Emilio had their fight, and Santiago decided to announce his girlfriend by showing up on the red carpet premiere of her movie in New York City.

I guess I haven't been honest with either of them, since

Carmen totally didn't know that Daniela and I dated in high school.

As of right now, she's under the impression we only met when I took her to her modeling casting. Santiago knows that we dated, and I think he's somewhat aware of the fact that we are trying to get back together. He's always been very intuitive, so it wouldn't surprise me that he knows something is going on.

"Daniela, do you know what's going on between them?" I say as Daniela walks into The Enchanted Ivy. I haven't seen her all evening, and just as I finally caught a glimpse of her, she was chasing Brooklynn, Santiago's girlfriend, out of The Enchanted Ivy, looking as though she was trying to speak to her. Which is exactly what I wanted to do with Santiago, but he has already left, too.

"Not really, no. She said they're fighting, but she wasn't right open with the details. Which is fine. I just wanted to be there for her." Daniela says, motioning back at the door Brooklynn disappeared out of.

"I'm sure they're probably fine, but after Santiago left for New York with her, I haven't had a chance to talk with him about their relationship. I'm not saying that it's necessarily my business, but I want to be there for him, you know?" I say.

"That's understandable, Matteo. I met Brooklynn at my first party back here, and just talking to a girl who reminded me so much of myself at her age was refreshing. We've talked almost every time that we've been here the same time." Daniela says, her eyes moving to Carmen and Alessandro. "Oh, are they a thing now? Officially?"

"What do you mean officially?" I say, raising an eyebrow at her choice of words.

"Oh, like you didn't see that coming. I've noticed those two eyeing each other these last few weeks. I think I might just be too intuitive, sometimes." Daniela says, her eyes once again moving back to Carmen and Alessandro.

"Well, I just learned about them a few days ago, too, so you're not that far behind me," I say, with a chuckle.

"Really? You didn't know that they were together?" Daniela asks quizzically, as though there's no way I didn't know they were a couple.

"I guess I've been busy thinking about other things," I say, stepping closer to her. "Other people." Daniela immediately smiles at this, and my face mirrors hers.

"Oh? Who are those other people?" Daniela asks, stepping closer to me this time. "Anyone in particular?"

"Well, I should have said someone." I'm unable to keep my grin masked when Daniela's nose scrunches ever so slightly as her smile widens. "She's all I've thought about since the day I met her." Daniela's teeth graze her lower lip as she listens, and it immediately widens back into a smile as I finish speaking.

"Maybe this person has thought about you every day since then, too." She says teasingly, lifting her fingers to my cheek. "Maybe this person-" Daniela breaks off and removes her hand as a chorus of laughter bursts around us. The birthday being celebrated is in full swing, and while no one seems to notice us, the uncertainty in Daniela's eyes is unmistakable.

Reaching down, I take the hand she dropped, and enclose it in my own. If she's not comfortable being so open about our affections for each other, then I'm happy with that. I'm happy with anything to do with Daniela.

Her eyes meet mine in a silent thank you, and I resist the urge to bring her hand to my lips. Instead, I settle for a gentle squeeze of her hand.

CHAPTER 32

Daniela

"How is Rena doing? Is the medicine working?" Matteo asks as we stroll through the hallways of The Enchanted Ivy. While he would've asked those questions anyway, his deeper worry for her is suddenly apparent. My mind races to all of the times he's asked about her since I've been back, and a small smile finds its way to my face.

"She's doing really well. In these four days, she's turned such a corner." I reply, glancing up to meet his eyes. "Maybe next week you'll have time to come visit her?"

Matteo's eyes flicker in slight surprise, but he immediately nods his head. "I would love to see you both next week. I can also bring anything you might need, too. If Lorena needs help with her garden, or anything else, I'm happy to help." He offers, sincerity in his voice as he speaks.

"Really?"

"Really. I enjoy helping out, and I know that it's just the two of you there, so some of it might be overwhelming for you." Matteo answers easily.

"Thank you so much. If I'm being honest, there's some sort of leak under the kitchen sink, but I haven't been home during usual work hours, so I haven't had anyone out to look at it. Maybe you know how to fix that?" I chew my lip, knowing that this makes me sound like an unkept person, but also that Matteo will understand.

"That should be easy, Daniela. Don't worry about it."

"You're kind of amazing, Matteo," I say, giggling a little as I finish speaking. "Just a little bit, though." Instead of teasing me back, Matteo just smiles even more.

"Maybe this is going to ruin the mood, but who is that Ryan guy that you've been out with?" Matteo suddenly asks, sounding both curious and like he doesn't want to broach the topic. My feet still, and suddenly my tongue no longer works.

"He's..." How can I explain this to him? How will I explain this to him? I can't go on lying about Ryan, since it's only a matter of time before Matteo sees some internet headline about me and Ryan together. I also know that surely this topic will be brought up if we continue down this path of a relationship. "He's a friend from college that was been wanting some help with his design business." I finally say. It's close to the truth.

"Oh," Matteo says, as though he doesn't really think this is the truth, but also doesn't want to just say he doesn't believe me. "How long is he going to be in town?"

"I don't know, actually. Probably less than a few weeks, I think." I answer honestly. I don't think Ryan has told me about any departure plans, but the sooner, the better. I haven't really asked him about it."

"Well, that's nice," Matteo says, as though he isn't sure

what else to respond with. I wouldn't know either, but at least he's trying to be supportive.

"Yeah, it will be nice to have my time back," I say teasingly, trying to lighten the mood. Although I'm sure I just did the absolute opposite.

"What do you mean?" Matteo asks, his eyes growing with curiosity.

"I meant I spend a lot of time with him, so it would be nice to have more time for myself," I say, trying to brush it off.

"Well, in that case, I'm excited for you to have your time back, too," Matteo says, grinning as he speaks.

My eyes search his, and for a moment, I'm tempted to kiss him. The feeling is overwhelming, but I know I can't. Not right now. I have more things to work out in my life before I do something extreme. Matteo seems to be thinking the same thing I am, and I avert my gaze, not wanting to give him the wrong impression.

When will this end? I need to be back to my normal life, without health problems, Ryan demanding, and the uncertainty of my relationship with Matteo.

I like to think of myself as someone who is strong, brave, and not easily overwhelmed. These last few weeks have been really testing me, and every time I think that there's a light at the end of the tunnel, it seems to disappear. Looking up in Matteo's eyes, I see that light returning, and it excites me for our future. I think we both know that what we have is special, and that we need to protect it.

CHAPTER 33

Matteo

Santiago strides out of my room, and I run my hand over my face. The relationship between him and Brooklynn is much more complicated than I initially thought, but I'm proud of how he's handling it. He's taking accountability for the fact that he hurt her, and will do everything to fix it.

I opened up to him about what's going on with Daniela, and he seemed somewhat surprised. When I told him about the situation with Daniela and Ryan, and mentioned that I haven't told her outright that I love her, Santiago's immediate response had been to tell her, and that completely shocked me. Santiago has never been forthcoming with his feelings, and this is the most he's ever spoken about them. Brooklynn has completely revived a part of him that has been gone. Well, if it was ever there to begin with.

The thought of outright telling Daniela that I'm still in love with her is somewhat terrifying, since she still hasn't been completely honest with me about Ryan—even if I don't know exactly what's going on—and the fact that she's still holding back from me. Of course, I understand that she is stressed and under a lot of pressure, which is why I don't want to rush her. But I feel as though, if I don't do something soon, she's going to move on with someone else. That someone else, possibly being Ryan.

Don't get me wrong, I don't hate the guy. I just don't like the idea of Daniela being with anyone other than me. I actually can't even stomach it. Daniela has been my one and only for years. Years of unconditionally loving her, without so much of a glance and another woman's direction.

After a few hours of staring into space, at my desk, I finally decided to lay in bed, but sleep doesn't come. I spend hours rolling around, hoping to fall asleep, and wash the uncertainty of my current situation.

Maybe this would be much easier if I didn't love her so much. But that's not an option. I love her so much that I almost *can't* tell her. The idea of her telling me she doesn't love me back as terrifying, but the more I think, about Santiago advice, the more I realize that he's right.

I've never been too shy about my feelings, but I know that I haven't been as open as I could be with them, since Daniela's been back.

I broke her heart. I shouldn't just expect that she's back, she's going to welcome me to open arms.

When I'm at her house tomorrow, I'll ask her on a date, and then I'll tell her I love her.

"Oh, it's so good to see you, Matteo." Lorena says from the couch as I step through the doorway.

"It's slowly to see you too, Lorena." I reply, giving her a smile before glancing down at the items in my arms. "I'll come see you in just a few minutes. Daniela is going to show me where to drop this stuff off."

Daniela is smiling, and her curls bounce behind her as I follow her into the kitchen. Her long skirt reaches just above her ankles and swishes there when she spins to face me. "This is the first time in a while I've seen you in something other than a tuxedo." She comments, look me up and down before reaching out and taking the bag from my hand.

"Hopefully it's not a fright." I tease, placing a small tool bag from my arm on the floor. "And, I could say the same about you. It's been a while since I've seen you in anything other than formal wear." I say, eyeing the long skirt, simple, sandals, and fitted sleeveless shirt she wears.

"Definitely not a scare, but somewhat unfamiliar." She admits, and it hurts my heart to realize that it's been so long since we've been around each other under normal circumstances. Under circumstances that people who are more than just acquaintances, see each other under. "I guess that's true. What do you think?" Daniela asks, spinning, lightly to show off the floating white fabric of her skirt.

"I think it looks beautiful. *You* look beautiful." My words ring with honesty, and her smile is enough to show me that she is still affected by me. It shouldn't make me as giddy as I feel, but it's another step in the right direction.

"I think you're mistaken about that. Thank you, though." Daniela says softly, brushing a few curls behind her shoulder as she opens the bag she took for me. "Oh, Matteo, you didn't have to get desserts."

"I'm not wrong about that. I may be wrong about many things, but about you, I've never been more sure." I respond, my words, betraying a deeper meaning behind my statement. Daniela's cheeks immediately become an even darker shade of red, and for moment, the sight of her in normal clothes, opening a grocery bag that I brought in, and in the kitchen with me makes me long for a world in which this is my every day. A world where this is normal for us. "Also, I know I didn't have to get sweets, but I wanted to. Hopefully, you like them. They're mango flavored." I say with a wink.

"Is it a coincidence that they're mango flavored?" Daniela asks with a raised eyebrow as she lifts the fruitcake from the bag and places on the counter, and then pulls out the box of chocolate, setting it next to the cake.

"No." I answer honestly, and her hands freeze on the refrigerator door for a second. "I seem to remember there's someone here who loves mangos more than any other fruit."

"Oh, really? Does this person have a name?" Daniela teases back, resting her hand on her hip after closing the door. She leans against the counter, looking through her eyelashes to meet my eyes. My heart quickens, but I force myself to calm down for just a second to come up with the coherent response.

"She goes by Daniela Lozano," I say, with a wink, stepping closer to her. I'm not sure what my plan is, but the magnetic pull between us is too strong to ignore.

"Well, Matteo Alvarez, your sense of memory is impeccable." She responds, reaching out to brush her hand across my left shoulder. "Although, the threads on this shirt, aren't." She teases, pulling her hand back to smooth down her skirt.

"Oh no, have I offended the worldwide famous fashion designer?" I ask, chuckling as I speak.

"With your dessert?" She pretends to think about this, but a smile breaks through. "No, not with that. However, your fabric choices, maybe."

"My apologies, ma'am. I'll be sure to not do it again." I say with a wink, receiving a smile from Daniela at this.

CHAPTER 34

Daniela

"Matteo, you look older in just these last few weeks. What has aged you so much?" Rena asks Matteo as he leans down to give her a quick hug and a peck on the cheek.

"Rena, that's not too polite," I tease, crossing my arms and stepping backwards. My skirt swishes at my ankles, the cool breeze flowing through the open windows stirring it. A quick chill runs up my exposed arms, and I reach for the cardigan sprawled on the back of the couch.

"It's just the truth, Daniela." Rena chides, patting Matteo's hand as he chuckles. "I am happy you came to visit me, though, dear."

"I'm happy to see you, too, Lorena. Daniela has told me that you've been keeping up with your telenovelas. Are there any I should watch?" Matteo asks, sitting next to her on the couch as she continues her grip on his hand. A swell of endearment grows in my chest as Matteo interacts with Rena. Of course, he's always been a gentleman, but knowing that he took care of her while I hid from my problems, and still cares about her even though I'm here, is special.

"Yes, yes, I need to tell you all about the one I'm watching. The heroine is from the States—her mother is from Mexico—and the boy she's falling in love with is the son of a billionaire." Rena excitedly says, her face wrinkling as a full smile takes over her cheeks. I can feel a smile of my own creeping up as Matteo matches her energy and excitedly nods along with her. Surely, he's not too interested in her telenovela, but he's interested in Rena's excitement.

"Really? Why can't she be with him?" Matteo questions, as though this is the most important question in the world.

"Well, the problem is that it's her new best friend's brother," Rena says with a gasp, as though this is the most scandalous confession she's ever made.

"No," Matteo mirrors her horror, and I can't help the burst of laughter that escapes me. They both turn to me, and suddenly I feel as though I'm a child about to be scolded.

"Daniela doesn't understand these things," Rena says dismissively. "I told her that you two need to date again so that she remembers what love and scandal feel like." She says easily, producing a choking cough from me, and a smile from Matteo.

"Rena!" I yelp, lifting my palm to my lips to conceal the burst of laughter threatening to escape me. "Maybe it's time for you to go back to your telenovelas and leave the real world alone."

"Oh, nonsense, Daniela. I'm just speaking the truth." Rena responds with an exaggerated roll of her eyes. "Right, Matteo? What do you think?" My face heats into a blush as my eyes meet his, and instead of even looking mildly embarrassed, he's smiling.

"I think we'd need to test that theory before saying anything for certain," Matteo responds to Rena, but his eyes stay on mine the whole time, sending a whole new flush to my cheeks.

"Okay, enough is enough." I exclaim, standing from the couch. "Matteo, you have a sink to fix and plants to move, and Rena, you have medication to take and food to eat."

"I don't get any food?" Matteo teases as he stands.

"Maybe after you're done with housework," I reply, brushing past him. "Rena's medication is on a strict schedule, and she needs to eat with it," I explain, leading Matteo back into the kitchen and sliding the pot of soup off the hot burner and onto a cool one.

"Don't worry about it, Daniela," Matteo says easily, leaning against the kitchen counter as I plate Rena's food and prepare her medicine. The feeling of his eyes on me as I work is both comforting and unsettling. "You're really good at that, you know?"

"At what?"

"Caring for her. You have this instinct and gentleness about you." Matteo answers. My hands stop for a moment, his words fully settling in.

"Do you really think so?" Every now and then, I have this terrible feeling that I'm not doing enough for Rena, but just hearing Matteo say that is almost like confirmation that I'm doing well.

"I know so. You've taken much better care of her than anyone else could, and you're happy to do it. She's lucky to have you here for her." Matteo responds, his tone full of sincerity.

"Thank you, Matteo," I say, moving past him as I deliver Rena her food.

She eats it rather quickly, and once she's finished, I help her to the downstairs bedroom and help her settle for a nap.

Matteo's back is facing me as I step into the kitchen. He seems to be focused on the photos that adorn every inch of the refrigerator and the wall around it. "Which one are you looking at?" I question, stepping closer to him. I immediately freeze, my eyes focusing on the picture he can't tear his eyes from. It's one of us at a high school dance, and we look happier than we've ever been. His arms were wrapped around my waist, and my hand was on his chest.

"I didn't know that she kept all these photos up," Matteo says, searching over the various photos. "I assume that she mustn't have let you pull them down." He says softly, his finger reaching up to point out a photo of us in sweatpants and sweatshirts in the backyard, sprawled out on a blanket.

"Nobody ever touches Rena's photos," I say, standing next to him now. "How come you didn't see these all the times you've been over?" I ask.

"I never spent much time in the kitchen. Usually, she would need help in the yard, or just bring things in the door, to the living room. I never studied these." Matteo answers, his eyes moving to a photo of both of us, my parents, and Rena. "I've always wondered where this went. I remember taking it—well, having a camera on timer, and running back next to you—but I never had a copy of it." He says, his eyes lingering on the photo for more than a minute.

"Well, it's been here. Rena takes her photos very seriously." I say, trying to lighten the mood.

"I see that," Matteo says softly, gazing over each and every photo like he wants to commit them to memory. "Do you think she has copies of any of these? Or would she be open to copying them?" He asks as he reaches a photo of him and my dad, standing next to each other like father and son, Dad's arm around Matteo's shoulder. My throat tightens as I remember the moment when the image was captured. We were hosting an outdoor dinner, and my dad was teaching Matteo how to cook the perfect steak, and I snapped the photo of them just before one of the steaks caught fire. I chuckle at the memory, and Matteo must be remembering it too, because he joins in.

"She probably has a digital collection of them all, and if not, I'm sure she'd allow you to have them copied." I finally respond. Matteo is in most of these photos, and up until right now, I didn't realize how much of a part of my family he was. Of course, I remember him being around all of the time, but just focusing on the dozens of photos where he's happily involved with us brings back wave after crashing wave of memories. Matteo was my first and only boyfriend, and this wall really displays that.

"That would be amazing. I'd love to have some of these at my house, and maybe create a wall like this." Matteo says softly, and I can tell he's just as choked up with memories as I am when his eyes land on a photo of my parents, smiling as they hold me at just three months old. "I miss them, you know?"

"Me too." I say softly.

"They were like the parents who actually enjoyed being

within my vicinity," Matteo says with a smile. "Even if they were frustrated whenever I'd be back with you a singular minute after your curfew." He's chuckling now, and a smile rises on my cheeks as I remember all of the talking-tos that we endured. Matteo and I were never up to trouble, but we'd spend hours talking and just lose track of time.

"They were never actually angry about it, you know?" I say, reaching over to brush my fingers against his knuckles. "My mom told me that they just wanted you to remember that they were my parents, and you didn't need to get too comfortable breaking the rules," I say with a small laugh.

"So, all of the times they said they were going to reduce your curfew by another hour, they were just joking?" He asks.

"That was totally a scare tactic," I confirm. "They didn't want us to be out hours after curfew or anything, but they didn't care about five, ten, fifteen minutes. They really loved you, Matteo." Matteo presses his lips together, and I know he's feeling all of the emotions I feel whenever I think about them for too long.

"I really love them, too," Matteo says softly, and I catch how he says love instead of loved. It's small, but the difference means something.

"Me too. I know they're up in heaven, though, and I know that they're glad we still have Rena." I say, finally wrapping my fingers around his. It sends goosebumps up and down my arms, but I'm glad to have been the one to initiate the contact between us. Matteo was always worried about pushing my boundaries—he was way too much of a gentleman to, but it was a constant worry for him—and I want him to know that I want this. I want us. Maybe I don't have all of the answers, but just standing in silence and staring at the memories of when life was much easier is a start.

"Is right here, okay?" Matteo calls out from the lawn. Rena gave me specific instructions on where she wanted Matteo to move her plants to, and I glance down at the little map she created before responding.

"Yes, that's the spot," I call back, using my hand to shield the sunlight as I watch him carry the heavy plant across the lawn. Rena likes her garden and plants to be periodically moved to best serve them with the sunlight and shade they need. "Those pink flowers need to go to that side, by the way."

"No problem," Matteo says back, easily lifting the pot that I was unable to move an inch last week. It must weigh at least a hundred and fifty pounds. Matteo's relaxed willingness to help this afternoon reminds me of the many times he would help my father with mundane tasks. While my parents were wealthy enough to hire cooks, cleaners, and landscapers, they never indulged in things like that. They never enjoyed the idea of hiring people to do everyday tasks that everyone should do.

The idea of having strangers in our home as we went about our daily lives always seemed like something strange to them, and in turn, it's never crossed my mind to hire someone to do these chores. Although, I strongly considered it last week when I couldn't move that pot.

"That's perfect, Matteo," I call out, giving him a thumbs up as he strides back over to the porch, where I'm currently watching him from. A few droplets of sweat bead his face, but since the weather is somewhat chilly, he's surely not too warm in his jeans and sweater.

"What's next on my list?" Matteo asks easily, stepping even closer to me, so that our bodies are a mere foot apart. "I know you said kitchen sink, but wasn't there something else?" His simple question of asking what else he can do for me sends my heart beating wildly.

"Well, there's the sink, and then if it wouldn't be too much, I kind of need my office rearranged." I stammer, the sudden closeness of him sending my mind racing.

"That's not a problem. What if I do the sink first? That way, I can spend as long as needed helping with the office, since you might need to have it moved around multiple times?" Matteo offers.

"That sounds good. After all of that, I'll make us dinner, if you'll stay?" I ask hesitantly, unsure of how long he's obligation-free.

"I would love that, but don't feel as though you need to repay me with dinner or anything, though," Matteo says.

"Oh, that's not why I said that. I just...I just wanted you to stay longer."

"In that case, I would love to stay," Matteo says, his eyes dropping down to my lips before quickly bringing them back to my eyes, as though he's unconsciously lowering them. "If we're done out here, let's move to the sink."

"Yeah, of course," I say, hating that my voice is becoming breathy. Matteo opens the door and holds it open for me, then follows me into the kitchen. "I'll clean out the soaps and stuff down there, and then you can take a look." I offer.

"Don't worry about it. I'll move them out of the way." Matteo says, sauntering to the sink before dropping to his knees as he looks inside the cabinet. I pull one of the barstools out and move it into the kitchen before taking a seat. Sure, I could sit on the other side of the counter, but the magnetic pull between us is too strong.

"Well? What do you think is wrong with it?" I ask after a minute of Matteo inspecting all of the pipes.

"It looks like I just need to tighten this connection, and that should fix the problem," Matteo answers. "Do you mind passing me that bag?" I glance around and quickly locate the small tool bag he's referring to.

"Here you go," I say, placing it in his hand. He removes a wrench, and within a few seconds, he's back on his feet, and...doing the dishes? "What are you doing?" I question, stepping over towards him, confused as to why he's washing the dishes I used to make Rena's soup.

"Oh, I'm just checking to make sure this is the problem, and that I've fixed it," Matteo responds, rinsing off the bowl he just washed, then placing it on the drying mat I have placed next to the sink.

"Here, I'll do that. Don't worry about doing the dishes, since you've already done the yard and fixed the pipe." I protest, pulling a handful of hair into a bun as I bump my hip into his, as if this will push him out of the way.

"Technically, the pipe isn't fixed, since I haven't tested it yet. Meaning, I should do the dishes." Matteo says lightly, placing the next dish on the mat.

"You're really good at coming up with excuses, Matteo.

You should have pursued a career in law." I comment, folding my arms and leaning against the counter.

"As if." Matteo scoffs, placing another dish on the mat. "I think I'm happy where I'm at right now, and even if I wanted something else, something tells me I'll be taking over the business soon."

"Why do you think that?" I inquire.

"I just think that my father's health is declining—you know he's in his sixties already—and as of late, he's been struggling to make it through the easier tasks without needing help," Matteo answers honestly, his voice the epitome of calmness.

"Are you worried about him?" When my parents passed, it was so sudden. There wasn't time to prepare or say prolonged goodbyes. What must it be like to watch them age and see the slow deterioration of them? Would that be easier? Harder? With Rena, I've always thought she was old. As a child, you always assume that the adults in your life are much older than they are, and by the time you understand age, they're actually old.

"I mean, yes, I'm worried about him, but I also think this is somewhat of a natural pattern for aging. He's old, and I have to accept that. He and Mother were older when they had me, and even older with Santiago and Carmen. For them, especially Carmen, they're still under this impression that yes, they're aging, but they don't see the day-to-day deterioration in their health." Matteo says, his voice even, as though he's worked through this all in his head many times.

"I can understand that, I guess. When I was their age, my parents both seemed really young, so I know what they're feeling." I respond. I was barely seventeen when they passed, so right in between Carmen and Santiago's ages now.

"They were young, though," Matteo says softly. Up until today, it never occurred to me that their passing took much of a toll on Matteo. I'm not sure why I never considered the fact that he would miss them, too, but listening to him speak about them today has opened my eyes to the fact that he misses them. Matteo practically lived here while we dated, and my parents treated him as though he was their son.

"Yeah, you're right. Mom was thirty-six, and Dad was thirty-seven." I say, mentally calculating their ages. My parents got married at eighteen, and had me at nineteen. They both said that while I should always be careful about a relationship so young, sometimes you just know. "It's crazy to think that by the time they were my age, they had a three-year-old," I comment, imagining a smaller version of Matteo toddling through the kitchen, playing around us.

Wait. Where did that come from? Did I just imagine a mini version of Matteo as my child? What is wrong with me? Why am I imagining our future children?

"It is pretty crazy to think about." Matteo agrees, placing the last dish down before facing me. "I think you turned out all right, though. So maybe what they say about having kids young is wrong."

"You think I turned out alright? You don't know?" I say indignantly, placing a hand on my chest as I pretend to be offended.

"Well, there are still a few more years before your frontal lobe is fully developed, so I'll give you my answer then. Until you're twenty-five, I'll give you an A." Matteo teases back, dropping to his haunches.

"Well, I guess I'll give you your final grade at twenty-five, too." I huff.

"It looks like this is all good, so now we can move on to your office," Matteo says after inspecting his work under the sink.

"Thank you so much," I say, bouncing on my feet at the sight of Matteo standing and brushing off his hands. I don't know why, but seeing him in my kitchen fixing things and doing the dishes is having a crazy effect on my heart. "My office is right down here." My sandals softly click on the hardwood floors as I lead him down the hallway into my space.

"Wow, this is quite the setup," Matteo comments as he follows me into the room. As he gazes around the room, I can't help but watch him. I don't think I've ever been this comfortable around another man, and as I take in our surroundings, I think about how uncomfortable I would be with anyone else here with me alone. With Matteo, I'm more than comfortable with him being alone with me, and I've never once worried about him doing anything rude or domineering.

"Thank you. It should look even better when we're done." I reply, stepping over to the desk that's covered in designs and doodles.

"This is really pretty," Matteo comments, picking up the design that currently has me in this whole mess.

"You think so?" I ask absently as I move the piles of pencils and markers into the drawer.

"I really love it, actually. When will you be releasing it?" Matteo asks, gently placing it with the other designs in the folder it was resting on before.

"Oh, I'm not sure yet. It's not done, and I've had some… issues with it. Probably next year. There will be another small launch in December, but I don't think this dress will make the cut for then." I say, not wanting to divulge all of the issues I've had with it.

"I can't wait to see it," Matteo says, closing the drawer and stepping back. "Do you want this moved? What's the plan?" I quickly relay the plan to Matteo, and once he understands it all, he begins quickly and efficiently moving everything.

Once it's all how I envisioned it, we move back to the kitchen, where I direct Matteo to a barstool on the opposite end of the counter. I begin to pull ingredients out of the refrigerator, and it's not long before I have everything to make my baked salmon, rice, and vegetables.

"Do you need help?" Matteo asks, standing from his chair to round the counter and begin washing his hands.

"Matteo Alvarez, if you don't sit down, you won't be eating at all. Let me cook dinner while you take a break. You've done yard work, handyman work, and interior design work. Let me handle this." I huff, setting down the knife that's poised above the bell pepper I'm currently slicing.

"Yes, but you helped with those things, so allow me to help," Matteo replies, reaching for a pepper.

"No, no, no. Take a seat, Matteo. I was the woman with the clipboard. You hauled about a thousand pounds of plants and furniture around, and even did my dishes. I want you to sit down and relax for a little bit while I make this." I say, shooing him around the counter back to his seat. "Besides, this will take me maybe ten minutes to prepare before I put it all in the oven and on the stove."

"If you're sure you don't need help-" Matteo starts, but I cut him off before he can even finish the sentence.

"I'm positive I don't need your help. I appreciate you offering, but really, Matteo, I have this under control and would like it if you were to sit there all nice and pretty and wait." I say, giving him a smile before returning to my work.

"So, you think I'm pretty?" Matteo asks, and I look up to meet his smirk.

"Of course that's the only thing you retained from all of that." I tease, mock rolling my eyes before lowering my eyes back to the food in front of me.

"You never answered my question," Matteo continues, and I can tell he's not going to drop this.

"Just a little bit." I finally give in, meeting his gaze to find that while his face still looks lighthearted, there's something deeper there, too.

"Well, I can say with confidence that you're the most beautiful girl I've ever seen, in case you were wondering." Matteo offers, not a hint of teasing in his voice anymore.

"Oh?" Is all I manage to make out, a flush heating my cheeks and neck. "Thank you, Matteo."

"You don't need to keep thanking me, Daniela. You don't need to thank me for feeling a certain way towards you." Matteo says softly.

"Well, I don't want to seem rude for just accepting everything you do over and over again without acknowledging it," I say, trying to come up with a good response for him.

"I would never think that you're rude," Matteo responds, meeting my eyes again.

"I'll try to remember that," I say softly, placing the tray

into the oven before turning back to Matteo. "But maybe you'll have to remind me every now and then."

Matteo smiles, and the only word I can use to describe his appearance is adoring. Everything about him screams love and gentleness, and while that terrifies me after everything I've been through, I can't help but be drawn to the pureness of it. I can't help but be pulled closer to him, no matter how hard I try to remind myself that this isn't the right time to try and grow our relationship.

Maybe I'm terrified of the idea that I won't be able to love him enough—as much as he loves me—and he'll soon realize that there are other people who can reciprocate the affection that flows from every fiber of his being. Especially right now, since I can't give every ounce of myself when I have a thousand other issues in my life. I'd be dragging Matteo down instead of uplifting him.

In high school, I never had that fear. Until my parents passed and we broke up, I never considered the idea that maybe I don't love enough, and everything I do is surface-level. Maybe I'm just not able to convey my feelings as eloquently as other women, and that's why I come off as cold and unfeeling, and why my circle of people has always been minuscule.

Right now, looking at Matteo, it's not hard to picture a future together. However, it's impossible to picture the road to forever. Matteo's eyes search mine, as though he knows I'm deep in conversation with myself, and instead of saying anything, he just continues to meet my gaze.

CHAPTER 35

Matteo

I park my car in the garage, but it's twenty minutes before I even muster up the strength to get out and walk inside. Spending the whole afternoon and evening with Daniela was amazing, and I want to do it again and again. I would be happy to live the rest of my life doing exactly what we did today, if it meant spending forever with Daniela.

Santiago brushes by me in the hallway, and his face is lit with a smile as he does so. He also smells like salt and the ocean, meaning he made the drive to the beach.

"What has you all happy?" I tease.

"Oh nothing," Santiago says quickly, but his smile betrays him, and I raise an eyebrow. "Okay, fine. Brooklynn told me she loves me, and we're completely official now."

"That's amazing, Santiago. It sounds like you were stressing about nothing last week." I say with a smile. Santiago nods excitedly, and I can't help but share his excitement. It sounds cheesy, but this feels like Santiago has finally started a new chapter of life. Over these last few weeks, there's been a difference in him, but it's finally completely noticeable. He's almost a new person, and the older sibling in me is almost bursting with pride.

"Well, I did need to stress because I hadn't fixed things between us, but now there's no need to stress." Santiago corrects me, reaching for his doorknob. "I might need to stress when it comes to planning dates, birthday presents, Christmas..." He says, trailing off as more events rush to his mind.

"I'm sure the dates part won't be that hard," I comment, trying to relieve his stress.

"Oh, but I kind of outdid myself tonight, and I don't think I'll live up to that ever again," Santiago says, running a hand through his dark hair. It has always been longer than mine, but it looks especially long right now.

"What did you do that was so out of this world?"

"Well, I took her to the beach, and I coincided it with this firework show, and it was this whole romantic gesture that might be difficult to top," Santiago explains. "Of course, I can do fireworks again, but it was paired with everything else, so that's kind of difficult to beat."

"Wow, that's quite something. I didn't know you were such a romantic. You must have got it from me." I joke, leaning against the wall, since it's obvious our conversation will last much longer than what I originally expected.

"Please. I just never used my romantic talents up until recently." Santiago says with a roll of his eyes. "What about you? You look rather happy right now, too."

"Daniela asked me to come over to her and Lorena's house, and while I was over there, I helped in the garden, fixed the sink, and then helped rearrange her office. We also ate dinner together, and afterward, I asked her on a date." I say quickly. Santiago's expression looks hopeful, and I can tell he's a little bit surprised to see all of that happened.

"That's really good, right? Did she say anything about that guy you said you've seen her with?" He asks curiously.

"Of course that's your only response," I say with a roll of my eyes. I've missed talking to Santiago like this. For so long, he's been reserved and tight-lipped about anything in his personal life. "But yes, she did. She said he's a friend, but something seems off."

"What do you mean?"

"I mean that I don't think she's saying he's a friend and she's actually interested in him, but I think there's something off with him. Like, he's not exactly a friend. I don't know how to explain it." I confess. "I know it sounds like I'm losing my mind, but I just can't place why it doesn't feel right."

"Well, maybe you should ask her?" Santiago says, as though this is the most obvious answer.

"I've tried, but whenever I bring him up, she tries to steer the conversation somewhere else."

"Hopefully it's nothing, then," Santiago says, checking his watch before glancing back up at me. "I know you won't understand, mister educated, but some of us have school in the morning, so I need to get to sleep."

"It must really suck to have just missed the age cutoff," I comment, knowing that he's always disliked being the oldest person in his class.

"At least I get the rest of the semester to go to school with Brooklynn." He says, as though this makes it better. "We're not in the same grade, but since she and Carmen are friends, and Alessandro and I are friends, we've started hanging out during lunch, and walking to most of our classes together."

"Oh?" It's rare that I wish to be back in school, but there are rare moments like this when I wish to be closer in age to my siblings. I was just about to graduate high school when Santiago was a first-year. "You're all cool together?" I've suspected that he and Alessandro rekindled their friendship since Carmen is dating him now, but hearing him sound happy about it is something I wouldn't have expected.

"Yeah, it was strange to see them together at first, but now it's more understandable, I guess. We all get along well, and since he and I have most of the same classes, and Brooklynn and Carmen do, it all works out for us."

"That's really good. I'm happy that you're all hanging out together. I haven't been around Carmen too often recently," I say, feeling guilty about it.

"She's just fine. I think she's a lot more independent than we've been imagining." Santiago says with a chuckle.

"That's good to know. Recently, I've been feeling slightly bad about trying to shelter her so much." I admit.

"Same," Santiago agrees.

"Well, it's good to know that you're both realizing how insanely overprotective you've been," Carmen says, startling us both as she opens her door and walks out into the hallway.

"How long have you been listening to us?" Both Santiago and I say at the same time.

"Long enough," Carmen says, folding her arms to lean against her doorframe. Santiago and I meet each other's gaze before returning back to Carmen.

"So, you just decided to eavesdrop without announcing your presence?" Santiago asks indignantly.

"I had to know what you two were talking about first. I remember all of the times you two would be whispering and then stop whenever I'd ask what you were talking about." Carmen says defensively.

"I don't really remember that," I tease, knowing full well we did that just to irritate her as a child. Carmen just raises her eyebrows in response, and all three of us burst out laughing.

"Back to the initial conversation," She says before returning her eye to mine. "When were you going to tell me that you and Daniela are a thing?" Right. She still doesn't know about the fact that we dated in high school.

"Well, we dated in high school, and then Mother and Father made us break up, and now she's back, so we're not exactly dating yet, but..." I trail off, unsure of what else to say.

"You what?" Carmen exclaims. "How come neither of you ever told me? I didn't know that you dated then. Much less dated Daniela Lozano." She says, completely bewildered.

"Carmen, I'm almost seven years older than you. It's not a surprise you didn't know about stuff like that. Besides, no one was supposed to know." I say pointedly at Santiago. This earns me a loud swallow from him.

"Why not? Why did they make you break up with her?" Carmen asks.

"Well, judging from your secret relationship, you know why. They didn't approve of it, and as soon as they found out about how much I loved her and her current situation, they made me break up with her." The harshness behind it still hurts, but Carmen just nods quickly.

"Wow. Why are Mother and Father so worried about all of that? At least you have a second chance with her now?" Carmen says, her questions piling up.

"They're stuck in the old ways of being more focused on a social status and a public image, more than anything else. Everything else could burn, and as long as they knew that they still were rich and famous, they'd be happy." I say, knowing it's the truth. "At least you two have the less intense version of them, and you both decided to jump out of the nest at the same time."

"Oh, come on, Matteo. I've had my fair share of disputes with them." Santiago says exasperatedly. "Carmen, too."

"Yeah, don't go getting on a high horse, right now." Carmen huffs.

"You two need to get some sleep. I know that there are classes to attend in the morning." I say with a smirk. "And here I was earlier thinking that it would be fun to attend school with you. You've both successfully changed my mind." With that, I slip into my room, leaving them both in the hall.

CHAPTER 36

Daniela

Just this one last outing with Ryan, and then I'm done. Free of his stupid plan, and free of his never-ending voice in my ear when we're out.

"I'll be back home later this evening, Rena," I say, stepping into her bedroom. "I'm grabbing dinner with a friend, but I shouldn't be out too late."

"Is it with that boy of yours?" She questions, eyeing my evening dress and makeup suspiciously.

"No, it's not," I say, and my voice must have sounded wistful, because Rena immediately begins speaking.

"You should tell him that you're ready to have a relationship with him again. I know he feels the same way." Rena says, reaching for my hand to pat it. "Stop being so afraid of your feelings. This will have its ups and downs, but you'll make it work. You're not complicated or too hard to love. Even if you were, I know that Matteo would still love you just the way you are."

"Rena, it's just that I don't know if I can give so much of

myself to a relationship. I want to. So badly." I admit. "I just worry that I'm not going to be enough, and even if I give it everything, I won't be able to give Matteo the love he deserves."

"Daniela, he loves you so much that he has enough love for ten Danielas. You love him so much, too. Stop worrying about not being enough, because you're more than enough. You loved him with all of your heart once, and I know you're going to do it again."

"The photographer is on the upper balcony," Ryan says, gesturing to the discreetly placed photographer.

"Okay," I say dryly. Every time I see Ryan, I wonder how I came into this stupid situation. When I stupidly ran outside of my date with Matteo, because I was still too heartbroken to control my emotions.

"You're in quite the cheery mood tonight," Ryan comments, taking a sip of his water.

"Maybe because I'm extremely tired of acting like this is a merry time for me, when in reality, I'd rather be anywhere else but here." I retort, tapping my nails on the table in annoyance.

"Well, remember you agreed to this." Ryan shoots back before pressing his lips together. "We can't be so loud. Someone will overhear us and jump to the wrong conclusion about this situation."

"And what would the wrong conclusion be? That you're holding me here against my will?" I hiss, finally meeting

Ryan's eyes. He seems shocked that I just spoke those words out loud, but he quickly regains his composure.

"Daniela, this is quite enough. I think we need to try to enjoy this meal as much as possible, and then move past this little dispute. How has your launch been?" Ryan says smoothly, with all the composure of someone who knows exactly how to direct and control the conversations.

"Slow down, Ryan. We're not moving past this, and I'm definitely not opening up to you about my personal or business life." I say, my frustration and anger rising with each word I speak. "And don't forget that after this, we're done. If I hear from you again, it'd better be a formal apology for this terrible experience."

"I wouldn't be so sure of that, Daniela," Ryan says with a panic-inducing chuckle.

"What do you mean?" I demand, my voice rising by two octaves. He surely doesn't believe that I'll willingly spend any more time with him, right?

"I'm just saying that women are usually all over me and never want to fully say goodbye. Besides, you'll be seeing much more of me when you're attending the launch of my new line next month." Ryan's ego seems to inflate with every word he speaks, and my irritation inflates right along with it.

"That was never part of my initial agreement. I will never-"

"What's going on here?" An all too familiar voice asks, as footsteps land in front of our table. Matteo.

"Who are you?" Ryan demands, indignant that someone would dare interrupt our argument. My heart swells at Matteo's appearance. I want out of this so badly, and more than that, I want Matteo.

"That doesn't matter. What are you doing?" Matteo's voice is dangerously low, and if someone were to be watching us, they would have no idea what's going on.

"What do you mean, what am I doing? I'm simply having dinner with my date, Daniela." At this, my mouth drops. I'm surprised Ryan doesn't recognize Matteo from that night a few weeks ago at my house.

"First of all, I'm not your date, and second-" I start, horrified at whatever he's insinuating.

"We're leaving, Daniela." Matteo says, stepping back to allow me to stand.

"No, she's not going anywhere with you-" Ryan begins before Matteo cuts him off.

"Choose your next words very carefully," Matteo says dangerously, his eyes darker than I've ever seen before. "You don't know who I am yet, but very quickly, you will realize that I'm someone you don't want to anger." With that, Matteo allows me to step ahead of him, but instead, I take his hand and walk next to him.

Sometimes, I forget that Matteo has approximately a billion dollars in his bank account, and enough connections to cover up just about any crime possible, but right now, I'm painfully aware of the damage he could do to Ryan. Ryan may be well-connected, but I doubt that few have as much power as Matteo's family does.

Matteo leads me to his car, and only once he's closed the door for me and slid into the driver's seat does he speak. "Did he hurt you?" I chew my lip, unsure of how to answer. Physically? No. Mentally? Yes.

"Not necessarily," I finally say. "I'll just tell you the full story, since you're now involved."

"I'd appreciate that," Matteo says, his voice and eyes a thousand times softer than they were with Ryan a few minutes ago. I explain the whole story, beginning to end, including the part where I was stupid enough to get in the car with Ryan. He listens to the whole story without displaying an ounce of frustration, and his gentle hand on mine as I speak is beyond comforting.

"I feel so stupid for ever trusting him, Matteo. When I got in the car with him when I was upset with you, I was being so stupid. I thought I knew him. That was what catapulted this whole plan of his into motion, and I feel so naive to have ever opened the door for this." I say after ending the story.

"Daniela, you can't blame yourself for this. You did know him, and he took advantage of that. He would have found another way to steal your designs and do this same exact thing had you never even seen him that night. If his true objective was to use you in this twisted plan of his, then there was nothing you could have done to change that." Matteo says reassuringly. "Do you want me to drive you home? Or do you need to eat?"

"Oh, well, I drove here, so I still need to take my car home," I say, even though the idea of driving home with Matteo feels like heaven.

"If that's what you're worried about, I can easily handle that." Matteo replies, giving me the opportunity to say no to him.

"If you're sure it won't be a bother to figure out bringing it home, then I'd love for you to drive me home," I reply, squeezing his hand lightly. With that, Matteo backs out of the parking spot he was in. "Why were you here to begin with?"

"I came to have dinner with the project manager for my house, since we're going over the final adjustments," Matteo says.

"Shouldn't you go back and talk to him, then?" I question, feeling suddenly guilty for pulling Matteo from his original plans.

"I'm going to call him when we get to your house. I was there an hour early, since I was already in the area. When I call him, I highly doubt that he'll even be on the road by then." Matteo says, reassuring me that I'm not inconveniencing anyone else's night.

"If you're sure that you're not going to leave him high and dry, then thank you, Matteo," I say, glancing over to him. The streetlights and passing cars illuminate Matteo's frame, and every few seconds, the occasional light will brighten his face.

"I'm positive that he'll be fine," Matteo says, glancing over to reassure me before moving his eyes back to the road.

Thirty minutes later, Matteo is pulling into my driveway and opening the car door for me. "Thank you so much, Matteo. Here are my keys." I say, allowing Matteo to walk me up the porch steps and to the door.

"I'm glad I was there for you, Daniela," Matteo responds. The illumination of the soft porch light makes his skin appear to be even more golden than it usually is, and I smile at the sight.

"I'm glad you were there, too. Things just got so out of hand, and-"

"Daniela, don't worry about it. Ryan isn't going to do

this to you ever again." Matteo says softly, stepping towards me to brush his hand along my cheek as he moves a stray piece of hair behind my ear.

"Thank you, Matteo. You truly are my knight in shining armor." I say, embracing his soft touch.

"I want to always be here for you," Matteo says gently, his gaze filled with love. "I hope that you'll allow me to be here for you every time you need help, or just someone to listen to you."

"I'd like that," I whisper, the sudden quiet around us much more apparent. "I should let you get going, though. I still want to go out with you tomorrow night, too."

Matteo smiles his breathtaking smile, and removes his hand from my cheek just before turning to go. "I'll be here at six. Your car will also be here when you wake up tomorrow."

I love you.

The words almost escape my lips, but instead of saying them, I quickly stand on my toes—thankfully, I'm wearing heels—and press a quick kiss to Matteo's soft cheek. "Thank you, Matteo," I say before turning and walking in the door.

CHAPTER 37

Matteo

After quickly calling my project manager to let him know that I won't be able to attend dinner, but that I just called in to the restaurant and changed the reservations for him and his wife, and that I put my card on file to prepay for their meal, I make a call to Santiago. I fill him in on the events of this evening, and ask if he's able to help me bring Daniela's car home. He agrees, and pretty soon we're on the road back to the restaurant.

"So, what are you going to do about this guy?" Santiago asks just before we reach the end of the drive.

"I'm going to have a nice talk with him, and he'll regret ever doing any of this to Daniela." I say, meaning each word of it.

"It sounds like you already have a plan, but if you need help, you can always tell me." Santiago comments as I pull into the spot next to Daniela's car.

"Thank you, Santiago. I think I have it all under control, but you're the first person I'll call if I need help." I say, stepping out of the car. "Here, you can drive my car behind me, and I'll drive Daniela's," I say, allowing him to slip into the passenger seat.

On the drive back to Daniela's house, a thousand scenarios play in my mind, but the end result of them all is clear. Make it clear that Ryan is never to come in contact with Daniela ever again, and that every article he had published is scrubbed from the internet. There will never be another connection between Ryan and Daniela as long as I have anything to say about it.

Very rarely do I try to remember that I have every lawyer and dollar at my disposal, but during a moment like this, I feel grateful that I'm able to use it in a manner of good for Daniela.

It seems like the drive takes only minutes to arrive back at Daniela's house, and after slipping her car key into the spot where Lorena leaves the spare key, I slide into the passenger seat of my own car.

"You don't want to drive?" Santiago questions as he backs out of her driveway.

"Nah, I think I have a pretty capable driver right now. I need to put your chauffeur services to work right now." I tease, resting my head against the back of the seat. Truthfully, I'm insanely tired and don't trust myself to continue driving. Especially since Santiago is with me, and not only would I be endangering my own life, but also his.

All day at work, I was fixing little mistakes Father made, and I must have spent at least two hours reworking the proposal he was about to agree to. Of course, I wouldn't let any business owner get scammed, but this is my own father. There's a certain level of pressure that comes with making sure he's not endangering his business. On top of that, I had my usual work, and then I was planning out tomorrow evening with Daniela.

"Hey, this isn't a free service, man." Santiago says with a chuckle as he weaves through traffic with the ease of someone who's done this many times.

"Well, it's not about to be free when you crash into something," I tease back. "What does your girlfriend have to say about your driving habits?"

"She thinks I'm an excellent driver, actually." Santiago replies, his eyes never leaving the road. "The trick here is to never lose sight of your surroundings. I don't think my eyes ever leave the road or mirrors when I drive." He says a second later, after he passes multiple cars in a row.

"That makes sense, I guess. What are you, my driving instructor?" I joke, fully taking notice of how his eyes actually never leave the road.

"You might just need one," He says, allowing the car in front of him to switch lanes. "With how slowly you drive, I'm surprised Daniela hasn't demanded to drive before."

"Hey, now. We both value our lives, actually." I say, mockingly. "You also didn't have to deal with Father tracking your car when you got your license to ensure that you never went a mile above the speed limit. You were given keys and a license and then turned free."

"That was probably for the best. Both of them would have had a heart attack by now if they knew just how wild I used to drive. This is tame." Santiago says easily. "Also, notice that I always keep both hands on the wheel, ensuring I never get too comfortable. Comfort makes you unintentionally less concerned about arriving in one piece at your destination."

"Wow, I guess you are my teacher now," I comment. He really is doing all of those things, and if I weren't analyzing the speed at which we're driving, I actually wouldn't notice how out of my comfort zone this is. "I might be able to understand where Brooklynn is coming from."

"What do you mean?" Santiago questions, sounding puzzled.

"I mean that you're not actually a bad driver, and you're rather careful, but in your own way. Nothing you've done is illegal or technically unsafe, and if I weren't paying so much attention to everything you're doing, I wouldn't notice how unlike me you drive."

"You sound like such a nerd, brother." Santiago scoffs, but there's a smile underneath it.

"You sound like you're a reckless driver, brother."

"What happened to nothing illegal or unsafe?" Santiago pokes.

"I take back my compliment. It's too late to keep it." I say, crossing my arms as Santiago drives through the gates to our house.

"Nah, I think I'm going to keep it." Santiago says, stepping out of the car. He tosses the keys over my car to me, and he does it over his shoulder.

"Show off!" I call out, and I barely make out his last sentence before the door closes behind him.

"At least I have something to show off."

CHAPTER 38

Daniela

The knock at the door pulls me from my last-minute adjustments to my lip gloss, and I rush to the door to meet Matteo. Upon opening it, Matteo is standing in front of me with a bouquet of flowers, and the world's most infectious smile to exist.

"You look so beautiful, Daniela." Matteo says, offering me the flowers. It's an assortment of my favorites, and just the thought of knowing that even though I haven't told him about my favorite flowers in years, he still remembers.

"Thank you," I say, stepping back to allow him to follow me into the kitchen. "I'm going to put these in water before we leave."

"I can do that for you, if you'd like." Matteo offers, extending his hand to take the vase. His hand freezes for a moment when I allow him to take it. "You still have this?"

The vase is one he gifted me on our first date, when he showed up with three different bouquets and a singular vase. There was a bouquet for Mom, Rena, and me. Along with my bouquet, he brought a vase that he must have searched far and wide for, because the initials M and D are in the glass.

"Of course I do," I reply, offering him the plant scissors. "You didn't expect I'd get rid of it, did you? This is one of my most valued possessions."

"I don't know what I thought happened to it. I just haven't seen it in so long that I was beginning to think it wasn't around anymore." Matteo says softly, making quick work of getting the flowers and the plant food into the vase. He moves to the sink to fill it with water, and as he does so, my eyes never leave him.

"Of course I kept it. I wouldn't dream of anything happening to that." I say, taking the vase from him and tracing the lettering with my nail. "My mom thought this was the most romantic thing ever, and always said that you should have bought a hundred more, because I would change out each set of flowers every time you brought me new ones, and every surface in the house had vases of flowers."

Matteo smiles at this, as though he's remembering all of the dates we went on. He never showed up to my house empty-handed and wouldn't dream of not saying a quick hello to my parents and Rena before leaving with me. "I guess I did bring flowers pretty often. The shop I bought them from knew me by name, and which flowers I had in my rotation. It's a shame they closed down." Matteo says with a chuckle.

"I don't think I noticed a specific rotation between them all," I comment, leaning against the counter to gaze up at Matteo.

"Well, there were seven different bouquets that were my go-to—unless you mentioned a specific flower around that time—and I would intentionally change out the order in which I got them in. I never wanted it to seem like it was just a habit for me, and there wasn't any thought behind it all. I just knew which ones were your favorites, and never wanted to bring you ones that you hated."

"Matteo, you did so much stressing in your teenage years, it's a wonder you're not gray yet." I tease, giggles escaping me. "Here I was, thinking that I had it hard with deciding what outfit to wear, when you were secretly working your flower rotation."

"Well, to be fair, clothing decisions can be stressful, too," Matteo says with a twinkle in his eyes. "Speaking of, how long did it take you to decide on this dress?"

My cheeks flush as I think of the embarrassing amount of time I spent going through my dresses. "Well, a rounded number would be two hours," I say, scrunching my nose at Matteo's teasing expression.

"Then it appears as though we're both back to our old habits." He says, offering me his hand. I love the way my hand slides into his and fits so perfectly in it.

"It appears so," I reply, locking the door behind us as we step onto the porch. "I forgot to tell you, but Rena is very pleased with your work out here. She told me to let you know that it's exactly what she wanted."

"I'm happy to hear that," Matteo says, opening the car door for me before closing it and moving to his side. "Even if a few of those plants were a real struggle to move and place exactly where she mapped out."

"She's so particular with where she wants them," I agree.

"But it all works for her, since she hasn't killed a plant in over twenty years."

"I can get on board with it either way. She deserves to have her way with something like where her plants are placed." Matteo hums as he drives.

"Well, I'm just glad you're able to make her plant dreams come true, because that was definitely not a job for me. I was able to move maybe two of them last week." I joke, and Matteo cracks a smile at this.

"Is that so?"

"Matteo, I barely made it across the lawn with the berry towers without toppling them all over. I chose them because they were the lightest, but then they were taller than me." I huff, remembering the hours out in the sun for just about now visible changes.

"Even one berry tower is more than nothing," Matteo says, meeting my gaze for a second before turning his eyes back to the road. "You'll never have to move a plant again, unless you feel like it." He promises, and at his words, a smile finds its way to my lips.

"I'll be sure to let Rena know that you've offered up your landscaping services indefinitely." I tease.

"That was amazing, Matteo. Thank you for dinner." I say as we exit the restaurant. My hand is in Matteo's, and instead of walking to the car, he leads us to the park that's nestled in the quieter part of the city.

"Thank you for joining me. I had an amazing time with

you." Matteo says, his voice slightly less stable than it was a minute ago.

"Is everything okay?" I ask as we stride down one of the paths. All of the trees above us are adorned with fairy lights, illuminating the path just enough to see, but not remove the magic of the night, either.

"Everything is more than okay. I'm just trying to figure out how to tell you something." Matteo says softly, stopping us under one of the large oak trees.

"What do you want to tell me?" I ask, stepping closer to him. We're barely a few inches apart, and the sparks between us are crackling and popping with every breath we take.

"I know that we don't have everything figured out, and that this might be early, but..." Matteo trails off before reaching up to brush my cheek with his cool fingers. Normally, the cold touch would send me reeling, but the warm flush that's worked it's way up my cheeks welcomes it. "I love you, Daniela Lozano."

My breath hitches, and instead of pulling away as I would have even a week ago, a smile creeps up my cheeks. "I love you, Matteo Alvarez." Matteo's eyes search mine for a fraction of a second before he pulls my lips to his.

The first gentle brush of our lips feels like I've been electrocuted, and my knees almost buckle from the sheer emotional rush that flows through me. Matteo's hands cup my cheeks as he pulls me even closer, and instead of feeling cool like they did just a moment ago, they feel like fire on my skin. My hand slips up his arm to wrap my arms around the back of his neck. A few stray hairs of his become entangled with my fingers, and if it's even possible, Matteo pulls me even closer to him.

Matteo's mouth presses even deeper into mine, and I gasp at the intensity and passion moving between us. After an unknown amount of time, Matteo pulls away from me, and we stand there for a moment, catching our breath like we just ran a marathon.

"I love you, Daniela."

CHAPTER 39

Daniela

"Hey, I have a question," I say as we drive back to my house. I'm not sure why it has taken me this long to consider this, but I suddenly feel very foolish about not thinking about it sooner.

"Go ahead," Matteo says easily.

"What if Ryan tries to retaliate on me since I left him at the restaurant last night?" I ask, nerves building within me as every worst possible scenario plays through my mind.

"He's not going to ever be a problem for you again." Matteo says simply, as though he just knows.

"How do you know?"

"Because he and I had a little...discussion and we mutually decided that it would benefit him to not associate himself with you ever again." Matteo says carefully.

"How did you get him to agree with you about that?" Last I checked, Ryan was more than ready to continue profiting off my hard-earned name.

"I'm a very persuasive man." Matteo replies, as though this is an obvious answer.

"Matteo, what did you do to him?" I question, feeling slightly strange that I have no idea what Matteo did to make Ryan leave for good.

"Do you care?" Matteo asks, sounding actually curious.

"Not about him, but I do want to know what you did."

"I just allowed him to understand that I have so many resources at my disposal, and there are thousands of people that I know whose only job is permanently removing things from the internet. He was also made aware of the fact that I have more lawyers than he can count, and if he'd like both his and his family's reputation to stay intact, he should remove himself from your life, and make it seem as though he never even knew you." Matteo answers, his voice cool as he speaks.

"Wow. And he agreed?"

"Not agreeing wasn't an option." Matteo says lightly, as though he does this every day.

"Thank you, Matteo. I should have asked for help or done things differently when this whole mess started." I say, genuinely meaning it. Why did I allow myself to be used in such a manner?

"You don't need to thank me, Daniela. I'll do anything you ask of me." Matteo says, reaching over to pick my hand up. "While I can agree that it would have been better to not go along with him at all, I know that you did it for the right reasons. You were worried about Lorena's health and the well-being of your reputation. People have to choose the lesser of the two evils, and that's the choice you were given."

"I know, but I still feel like I could have done things differently. If I hadn't-"

"Daniela, Ryan had already chosen you to help with this terrible plan of his, and one way or another, he would have found a way to put you in this position. You couldn't have done anything differently." Matteo says, cutting off my negative spiral.

"You're right, and I know that, but sometimes it's hard to feel the truth," I respond. Even though I sound like I'm crazy, I know Matteo gets what I'm saying.

"As long as you know the truth, that's what matters." He says, pulling into my driveway. "Let's forget about it all, since it's behind us."

"I'd like to never think about him again." I agree as Matteo helps me out of the car.

"Who are we talking about?" Matteo teases, leading me to the door.

"You're pretty great, you know?" I whisper as I wrap my arms around Matteo and pull him into a hug.

"I'd contradict that and argue that you're pretty great, but for the sake of the moment, since I know you'll argue with me, I'll stay quiet." Matteo chuckles into my hair.

"You're right about that," I say, inhaling Matteo's scent.

"Occasionally, I get some things in life right." Matteo says softly, this time more serious.

"Like what?"

"You."

CHAPTER 40

Matteo

"Matteo, I'm having trouble understanding this. Can you read it to me?" Father asks, lifting a paper to my outstretched hand.

"Father, this is your lunch order. What are you not understanding?" I say, quirking my eyebrows as I read it again.

"Is it? I could have sworn that I just had a letter from your mother in my hand." He says absently, moving papers around his desk, dropping random items as he does so.

"Father, are you okay?" I ask, suddenly realizing that something is seriously wrong.

"Of course I'm fine. Just help me find my lunch order so I can give it to my assistant." He huffs.

"Father, you just gave it to me. I'm calling a doctor. Wait here." With shaking hands, I call an ambulance for Father. Something is seriously wrong.

"Yes, he was experiencing early signs of a stroke." The nurse explains to me as we walk into Father's room. "We're going to start him on this medication, and it should definitely reduce the risk of another one. We recommend removing him from any type of mentally taxing jobs." She says, nodding as though she's explained this to many people before us.

"He'll be okay, though?" Mother asks anxiously from Father's side.

"Mr. Alvarez is expected to make a full recovery, yes." She says, checking the monitor next to the bed before excusing herself.

Carmen and Santiago are still at school since Mother refused to call them. She wants it to be less of a panic-inducing moment when she tells them, and while I don't fully agree with her, this is her husband and children.

"Matteo, I think it's time for your father to retire. We've been discussing it recently, and this is the push we need." Mother blurts out from next to the hospital bed.

"I've been thinking that him stepping down would be good," I comment, unsure of what to say.

"You're obviously going to take over," She hurries on, her mind racing a mile a minute. "I'm going to call Garrett right now to get the papers drawn up. Watch your father."

Garrett is the head lawyer for the business, and is always one phone call or text away for my parents.

"Matteo? What's going on?" Father asks, as he sirs. I move to the side of his bed and reach out for his hand.

"You had a mini stroke, and you're here in the hospital," I explain, giving his hand a reassuring squeeze. The doctors were quick to let me know that this was a very minor case, and that's the only reason I'm being so calm about this whole situation.

"Where is your mother?" He asks, glancing around the room.

"She went out to call Garrett, but she should be back in a few minutes," I say gently.

"Is this about me retiring?" He says exasperatedly.

"Yes." I don't even try to hide it from him, since Mother will undoubtedly tell him when she comes back.

"It was coming." He says with a shrug, since he knows that there's no use arguing with Mother. "You're about to be the top man there, Matteo. Are you excited?"

"Let's slow down a little bit, Father. I'm not excited that you're here and that I'm taking over because you're unhealthy. I do look forward to continuing to care for the business as you do, though." I finish as my own head starts to spin.

"Matteo! Why didn't you tell me he's awake?" Mother demands, rushing back into the room. "How are you feeling, dear?"

"I feel fine. How did your call with Garrett go?" And just like that, they're back to business, social status, and everything that should be at the very back of their minds right now.

"Matteo, the date is set. Tomorrow we're all going into the office and signing it all to you." Mother says, catching my attention. I nod, but for some reason, the rest of me feels behind. It must be the sheer suddenness of this all that's making me feel off.

"I know that there are certain safeguards in place to make sure no one in ill health is leading, but why is there such a sudden urgency?" I question. Maybe it's just that I feel we should be more worried for Father's health than the company right now, and that's why my mind is moving so slowly compared to Mother's.

"Yes, that's exactly why. The board will be in shambles if they find out he's had a health scare, and is unable to perform his usual tasks, and that there's no plan to remove him from the head of the company. This will be a gigantic battle unless you're immediately placed in charge. Which, Garrett is working on right now. You've been pre-approved, for lack of a better word, and once he has all of these drawn up, you'll be able to take full ownership from your father."

"Father said you've been discussing this recently. Why?" My mind is becoming clearer now that the imminent danger is gone. Father and Mother both meet each other's eyes before turning back to me.

"We've been talking a lot since Carmen and Santiago have become...open about their relationships and lives they're living, and it has become more apparent to us that we need to be here for our children. We've been less than exceptional in all of the ways that matter, and while we've provided any materialistic things they've wanted, we don't have a relationship with them." Mother says, her voice brimming with emotion.

"Well, that's exciting," I say, genuinely meaning it. "I'm sure it will be an adjustment for everyone, but this will be good for you all."

"That's what we've been thinking. Of course, it hasn't been extremely long that we've been talking about it, but seeing that all of our children are deceptive about their relationships made us realize that maybe we haven't been there in all of the ways they need. Is there another good reason as to why every last one of you has chosen to hide the fact that you didn't want us involved?" Mother questions.

"Do you want my honest answer to that question?"

"Why not? We've definitely made a lot of mistakes with parenting, and maybe you can give us some insight into why both of your siblings don't want to be open with us." Are the people in front of me actually my parents? The people I know would never in their lives have a conversation like this.

"I can definitely say that they both feared you wouldn't approve of their relationships and would...encourage a breakup," I say pointedly. Both of them wince and turn to each other before Mother starts speaking again.

"Matteo, I haven't felt ready enough to do this, but we're both sorry about what we did to you and Daniela back when you were teenagers." Mother says, sounding like she genuinely means it. "When we first saw her back here, it was a surprise, and I tried not to feel guilty. I know that was wrong, but I kept telling myself that I did it for our reputation, but soon that lie I was telling myself wasn't holding up anymore."

"Listen, son, we never wanted you to have your heart broken, or even to break hers. We just wanted what was best for you. When you never even looked at another woman again, we should have noticed that what we did was wrong, but we were stubborn." Father interjects, like he feels equally as guilty.

"He's right." Mother agrees. "Then, when I spoke to her a few weeks ago, there was this strange feeling where I felt like I was speaking to one of my own children."

"What do you mean?" I ask quizzically.

"She just seemed so young. Suddenly, I realized that if I feel she's young now, how would I have felt if I looked at her as just a teenager, back when we made you break up with her? In my eyes—this sounds wrong, I know—she was just a distraction in your life, and she wasn't just a teenager who was going through more than any person should ever have to." Mother says, a few tears prickling the corners of her eyes. "Then she said something that made me have this click in my brain when I realized she was barely older than Carmen at that time. How could I have been so terrible to a child barely older than the one I've tried to shelter all of my life?" Mother asks, sounding genuinely horrified with her past self.

"So, this is our formal apology, and I know that it won't ever take away the pain we caused both of you, but we needed to get this off our chests. We planned on trying to bring it up to you soon, but with everything happening right now," Mother says, gesturing between the three of us and the hospital monitor attached to Father, "we feel like this is the best time. We're sorry for making you break up with Daniela, for all of the terrible things we said about her and her family, and for making you the bad guy. Not only did we force it, but we didn't take any of the blame, and probably led Daniela on to think you were the one behind it all."

"I accept your apology and forgive you both," I say, thinking for a moment before speaking again. "Santiago and Carmen are both really happy right now, and this isn't exactly my place to say anything, but please don't mess up their relationships when you try to become more involved. I don't think you'd intentionally do anything now, but please be careful."

"We will be." Mother says, pressing her lips in determination.

"I guess since we're having a whole life discussion right now, it might be the right time to tell you that my house has been finished, and I'll be moving into it soon. It'll give you more time to spend with Santiago and Carmen, too." My heart thrums a little bit harder with excitement, but also a pang of sadness that I won't be able to see Mother and Father make an effort to grow their relationships with Santiago and Carmen. It's for the best that this is all happening at the same time, though. I know that if I stay, then I'll end up trying to mediate all of the interactions, and this is something that all of them need to figure out.

Once I started really working for Father, the relationship between us just grew naturally, even though we never really had one before then. Without trying, it made me much closer to both of my parents, and while I'd love to be friends with them, right now, they need to start working on the foundation of a relationship with my siblings.

Besides, I'm more than ready to move into my house. The building and designing have taken years, and it feels surreal that it's finally ready. Also, the only reason I decided to continue living with my family while I could have easily moved out years ago was because of my siblings. Now that Father and Mother are going to be spending more time with them, I don't need to worry so much about them.

"You are?" Mother asks, and it sounds as though she's trying not to sound disappointed.

"Yes. It's finally done, and I'm excited to move to my next chapter in life." I say, debating on telling them about Daniela. What's it going to hurt? "Since we're on the topic, Daniela and I have been back together, and I know that my future has her in it." The statement feels odd to say out loud, and I don't have a clear, definite reason for saying it other than I want them to know that regardless of whatever they did in the past—and how much work I had to put in to get my relationship back—they didn't completely destroy my chances with Daniela, since I can tell that's what they've been thinking this whole time we've been talking.

"Really?" Mother asks hopefully. "That's wonderful, Matteo."

"Thank you, Mother," I respond. Father also congratulates me, and for a moment, we're silent as they both seem to be considering something.

"Are you going to marry her?" Mother suddenly asks, not sounding like she has an aversion to it, but rather, she sounds hopeful.

"Well, I mean," I stutter, feeling off guard by the question. In my head, I've always known I'm going to marry her, but I've never voiced that to anyone. Especially not my parents.

"You should." Mother says, breaking the silence.

"Matteo, I'm so sorry all of that happened," Daniela says, squeezing my hand lightly as we walk the paths around the golf course in the crisp autumn air.

"He's okay, and that's what matters," I reply. Daniela hasn't said it, but I know that this is hard for her to hear me going through. "This afternoon, I'm going to visit the company and finalize everything to sign it all over to me."

"That's pretty exciting," Daniela says, her nose scrunching as she considers something. "Will this lengthen your work hours?"

"What do you mean?"

"Will you be even busier than you are right now? Since you'll be the owner?" Daniela asks curiously.

"I think since my responsibilities will be changing so much, that it might be an adjustment at first, but the actual work hours shouldn't change," I respond. For a moment, the only noise is the crunching of leaves underfoot.

"I'm glad." Daniela says, glancing up to meet my eyes. "I already work so much, and you working even more hours would be rather unfortunate. I like spending time with you."

"I love spending time with you, Daniela. No job or work obligation will take priority over you. I promise." I say softly, lifting her hand to my lips. I brush a soft kiss over it, lingering for a second before dropping it back down between us.

I want this. I want us.

"I want to spend forever with you, Matteo," Daniela says, meeting my eyes once more.

Daniela

Matteo's mother, sister, and brother watch as he picks up the pen to sign his name. It shouldn't feel ceremonial, since the business is just being passed down from his father to him, but I know how important this is.

"And we now have our new owner and leader of Alvarez Trade." Mr. Alvarez says, patting Matteo on the back as he steps away from the papers.

When he initially asked me to come, I thought that it might be strange to be around his parents, when they so obviously dislike me, but upon my arrival, his mother immediately pulled me into a hug and whispered I'm sorry. I know that she's referring to everything that happened when I was in high school, and when I pulled away a moment later, Matteo was watching intently. Did he arrange for her to apologize?

Matteo meets my eyes from across the table that seats his board members, and just the sight of him makes me smile.

His eyes are saying something that he's not, but I can't put my finger on it.

"My first order of business is hiring myself an advisor and assistant," Matteo says loudly enough for the room to hear.

"Yes, yes, you'll need to get something arranged." His father says, and in an instant, I know exactly what he's going to do.

"Santiago, it's time you became an official hire," Matteo says, meeting his brother's eyes before turning back to the group of board members.

"Really?" Santiago asks, glancing around as though there's another Santiago in the room with us.

"Really." Matteo says, motioning for him to step forward. My heart skips a few beats as he meets my gaze once more. "Thank you for being here." He mouths before more conversation and chatter start to fill the room.

"I'm really proud of you, Matteo. You're now some fancy business owner." I tease, and Matteo's face instantly morphs into a smile.

"As if I'm not eating dinner with Daniela Lozano. World-famous fashion designer, business owner, and the most beautiful woman on earth." Matteo responds, taking a bite of his sushi. Eating sushi after just signing your name to take ownership of one of the largest companies in the United States is probably frowned upon, but tradition is tradition.

"Today is about you, though," I say, taking a sip of water

and shifting on the blanket. We decided to eat our food at The Enchanted Ivy, as some sort of silly remembrance of us meeting here six years ago.

"No, today is about us." Matteo replies, his voice changing slightly.

"And why is that, when you're the one who just had a whole celebration?" I ask, eyebrows furrowing.

"Because I wouldn't be here without you, Daniela. I was the most awkward and shy person before we started dating, and there is no way I would have even had enough confidence to do any of this without your encouragement." He answers easily.

"That's not true, Matteo. You're smart enough that you would've figured it out by yourself. I was probably a distraction back then, anyway." I tease.

"Not at all. If you even want to consider yourself a distraction, then you have to know that you're the best distraction God has ever given me." Matteo replies, reaching over to take my hand in his. We eat in silence for a few more minutes before my earlier question comes back to mind.

"Oh, I have a question," I say, placing my utensils down on my plate.

"Go ahead."

"Earlier yesterday, your mother hugged me and told me that she's sorry. What was that about?" I ask.

"So that's what she said?" Matteo says. After I nod, he continues. "The other day, after Father's health scare, they both admitted to feeling terrible about everything they did to our relationship and us."

"Oh really?" Sometime in the last week or so, I stopped caring. I used to have this desire to know why Matteo broke up with me, and then after that, I was still hurting from knowing that his parents would think such terrible things about me. Sometime around when Matteo stood up to Ryan for me, I realized that none of that even matters, because it's the past. Nothing I can do will change it, and just like coping with the grief of my parents' passing, I had to accept it for what it was.

"They're both genuinely sorry, Daniela." Matteo says, pressing his lips together before speaking again. "At the time, I was so angry with them, but then somewhere along the way, I realized that it would be the last time they ever had so much control over me. While I will always regret listening to them, it might have been for the better that I did."

"What do you mean?"

"I mean that I will never choose anything or anyone over you again. It hurts to think about the four years we could have spent together, and I never want to spend that much time away from you again, but like I said earlier, I was so unable to stand up for myself. Now, I know that even if something tries to break us apart, I'll lose everything before I lose you." Matteo declares, and his reasoning finally makes sense.

"Oh, I see," I say, considering everything he's said for a moment. "I used to be so hurt over you breaking up with me, and it definitely changed the way I saw myself for a while, but I get what you're saying. If none of that had happened, I wouldn't have had that overwhelming urge to leave and make a name for myself. If I stayed here, I would've been too consumed by the memories of the city to take any steps forward."

"I'm never going to stop being sorry for that, Daniela."

Matteo says in the same regretful tone that always appears when he talks about our breakup.

"Don't be." A few minutes later, the rustling of leaves draws my attention to the tennis court that we used to spend countless hours at. "Don't you think it's crazy?" I suddenly say, filling the silence that has been surrounding us.

"What?" Matteo asks curiously, his eyes searching around us for what I must be talking about.

"That we met here, Santiago and Brooklynn met here, and so did Alessandro and Carmen." Earlier today, Carmen and I got to talking, and when she mentioned meeting Alessandro here, it reminded me of Brooklynn asking about Santiago when she was new to the city.

"I never thought of it like that, actually. You're right." Matteo admits, his eyebrows furrowing before speaking again. "There must be some sort of magic in this place. It will be quite the story to talk about a few years."

"Why in a few years?" Does Matteo think that we'll only still be talking about a future then? That we won't be married, or at least engaged?

"Well, it'll be at least two years before Alessandro will be able to propose to Carmen, and at least another one before they're married. Same with Santiago." He answers.

"So, you think both of them are going to marry them?" I ask curiously. It's not that I don't think they'll end up together—I mean, look at Matteo and I—but his certainty is interesting.

"We Alvarez are well-known for making up our minds and sticking to them. Especially, when it comes to love." Matteo says simply. "Did you know my parents met when they were in college, and didn't keep in contact for ten years, but still knew that they wanted each other?"

"You're joking,"

"Not at all. They dated for a year, but my mother moved to Spain for seven years, and my father was building a business. They broke up before she moved abroad, and while they dated here and there, they both still hoped that they would have a chance again. When they coincidentally met in an airport ten years later, my father asked her to marry him on the spot."

"No he didn't!" I exclaim. "This story sounds a little too much like a storybook."

"I'm being completely honest. They've both changed a lot since then, but I think with my father having that scare and all three of their children being in relationships, it reminded them that their relationship is the most important thing. Not their business or social status." Matteo says thoughtfully. "I also think that since I'm officially moving into my house, it's making their life more real. They don't have endless time with Santiago and Carmen, and it's an awakening for them."

"Speaking of your house, when do I get to see it?" I've been curious about it, since it's the one thing he hasn't been talking about recently, and it feels strange to know that I don't even know where he's going to be living in a week.

"We can go right now," Matteo says, standing to offer me a hand up. My green dress rustles in the light breeze as we walk back to Matteo's car. Just before I slip past him into the seat, Matteo wraps his arm around my waist and presses a quick kiss to my lips that feels urgent and full of nerves.

"Are you okay?" I ask once he pulls away.
"Of course." Matteo says with a smile. "I just love you."

CHAPTER 42

Daniela

"This is..." I suck in a breath as I stare at the white wraparound porch. "Is this real?" My brain searches for a mental image of the house Matteo and I carefully laid out. We always said that we were going to get married and have a house on at least five acres of land—enough space for our kids to run around—and we detailed out each and every space in the house, down to the white wraparound porch.

"It's very real, although every time I see it, I feel as though it's about to disappear from right in front of me," Matteo answers, taking my hand and leading me up the steps. "Would you like to do the honor of unlocking it? I haven't been here in a few weeks, so this will be the first time I'm seeing it finished."

"I'd love to," I whisper, taking the key and slipping it into the lock. It's as though I'm stepping right into a dream as we walk into the entryway. The first sign I see hanging is directly to the right of me, and the name Alvarez is written across it. "How long have you been working on this?"

"Well, including laying out all of the plans, three years. I started it the week after I turned eighteen." Matteo answers, gazing down at me while I look around in awe.

"I can't believe this," I say, tears prickling the corners of my eyes. "I love it in here." Matteo leads me through all of the rooms, both floors, and then finally we're back in the large family room.

"What do you think?" Matteo asks, holding both of my hands in his, his eyes just as emotional as mine.

"I think that I can't wait to spend the rest of my life with you," I whisper, glancing around the home that we designed so many years ago, when all we could do was dream about forever. Now, I can feel it. Within these walls and this city. Most importantly, I feel it in Matteo.

I know it in Matteo. I know how kind, thoughtful, and honest he is. How protective and gentle he is. No matter how long we spent apart, instead of losing himself, he continued to love me and worked towards a future he could only have faith in.

"Daniela," Matteo begins, lowering himself to one knee in front of me, his voice strong and sure. "I wanted to give you this as a promise ring four years ago, and even asked your parents' permission, and received their blessing to do so." Matteo begins, reaching into his pocket to pull out a delicate wooden box.

"When I asked your father for his blessing, he said that he couldn't ever picture you more in love with anyone else, and that as long as I kept the spark and passion for life in your eyes, I had his approval." Matteo says, taking a deep breath. "When I asked your mother for her blessing, her only condition was that even on our worst days, when the world felt like it was falling apart from beneath us, I would protect and care for you. That I would support you mentally and spiritually, no matter the battle, and that I would physically guard you from any danger. As long as I did those things, I had her approval."

"Matteo..." Tears are streaming down my cheeks now, flowing faster and harder than they have in years.

"And most recently, I asked Lorena for her blessing. Her only condition is that you never doubt my love for you. On our worst and best days, I will never make you question my love." Matteo says, breathing deeply before continuing. "I promise all of those things to you and more. So, Daniela Lozano, will you marry me?"

"Yes."

Daniela

"Okay, one, two, three!" Brooklynn calls out from the lawn. She's holding a portable camera pointed at my little family, and at the very last second, Matteo presses a kiss to my cheek. "That's perfect!"

I allow Alexandre to slip down my hip and run out in the yard to Santiago, who has been making funny faces behind Brooklynn's camera to keep the attention of the children. Adelaida squirms in Matteo's arms, and Carmen immediately rushes forward to take her. "Come to your favorite aunt, honey." She moves to sit with Alessandro on one of the swings, and he wraps his arm around her middle.

"Hey, I heard that!" Brooklynn calls from the ground with Santiago and Alexandre.

The birthday decorations around us are celebrating Alexandre's fourth birthday, but right now, it feels like more than that. Both of Matteo's siblings are married now, but we still spend so much time together, despite all of our busy schedules.

"You're so beautiful," Matteo says softly into my ear as he wraps his arms around my waist. "I'm so happy this is our life."

"Me too." I say, leaning my head into his chest. It's hard to believe there was a time when I didn't know Matteo. When I didn't have his comforting touch and reassuring words, anytime I needed them.

We got married just shy of a year after becoming engaged, and right after that, Rena and I moved in with Matteo. Ever since then, Matteo and I have been inseparable.

Matteo's parents and Rena are all seated on one of the porch swings, with Brooklynn and Santiago's three-month-old daughter, Arianna. While Rena isn't related to any of Matteo's siblings or their spouses, they've all spent so much time here at our house with her that she's practically a great-grandmother to their daughter, too.

My gaze moves to Carmen and Alessandro, and even though her stomach has just barely begun to swell in the early stages of pregnancy, I can't stop the smile on my face. She's already such an amazing aunt to Alexandre, Adelaida, and Arianna, and I know she and Alessandro are going to be amazing parents. All three of the cousins so far have been unintentionally named A names, but now I can't help but wonder if we're going to stick with it.

"Okay, everyone. It's time for cake! Who's ready?" Matteo's mother calls, stepping towards the table with cake and ice cream.

"Me! Me! Me!" Alexandre screams, rushing towards the stairs. Santiago quickly picks him up before the first step and safely sets him next to the cake line, giving both Matteo and I a quick wink. Alexandre is so full of energy, and we've had more than one excited misstep that has left him with scrapes, so going up the stairs is something we all try to avoid letting him do.

"Do you want chocolate, Carmen?" Alessandro asks Carmen as she waits for him to bring back her cake. In one hand, he's holding Adelaida, and in the other, he has two plates of cake. He makes it look easy.

Chatter flows around us as the people we love the most laugh and play with our children, and while Brooklynn just took a photo of my little family, I wish for a way to capture it all. The chocolate covering Alexandre's face, the grass stains on Santiago's pants from playing in the yard with him, the giggles coming from Adelaida as Alessandro tickles her arm, Brooklynn's infectious smile as she cuddles Arianna, Carmen's lively spirit as she teases her siblings, and Rena and Matteo's parents as they soak in the love between their children and their spouses, and all of their grandchildren.

Most of all, I want to capture everything about Matteo. He's so full of love, and true to everything he promised me, my spark and passion are stronger than ever. He's protected me in every way possible, and most of all, I've never doubted for one second that this isn't the life he wants. I know that he sees our children as the largest blessings in our lives, and that he never takes a second of anything for granted.

"I love you, Matteo," I whisper, pressing a kiss to his cheek.

"I love you so much more than words will ever describe, Daniela." He says, pressing his lips to the top of my head. "Thank you for being the best wife, mother, and best friend. I couldn't do this without you, and I wouldn't want to, either. I love you."

Stay Connected!

I hope you enjoyed Love and Legalities as much as I loved writing it! It would be amazing to hear your thoughts in a review on your favorite book retailers, review sites, and social media! You can find me on all social media platforms, as well as my newsletter.

- Jenevieve Hernandez

Acknowledgments

THANK YOU for reading Love and Legalities! It's so crazy to me that I'm finished with this series, and that this book is coming out two days before my one-year anniversary of publishing my first book. How is it that I have FOUR books out?

Thank you to my family for supporting and encouraging my love for telling stories, and for allowing me to talk about them for hours on end. You are all the best!

Thank you God for blessing me with the talent and desire to tell stories.

Again, thank you, dear reader. You're so loved and appreciated.

- Jenevieve Hernandez

About the Author

Jenevieve Hernandez is the author of sweet and swoony romances, filled to the brim with the feeling of falling in love. She loves portraying character growth, unique plots, and, of course, romance in her books. Her books will never contain any explicit content, and are always guaranteed happily ever afters.

She enjoys spending her time in the pages of books, traveling from one story to the next, or outdoors, exploring the world around her.

www.ingramcontent.com/pod-product-compliance
Lightning Source LLC
Chambersburg PA
CBHW021156010826
48971CB00014B/2217